GUMSHOE

MICHAEL COMPTON

Published by The Journey Press, Memphis, TN.

ISBN 10: 0996625402
ISBN 13: 978-0-9966254-0-1

-1-

Shadows and fog. A wedge of white light flickers at the end of a long corridor, floating towards me.

"Dead man walking," a guard says.

Am I? Walking, I mean? I can't even feel my feet, but I hear their scrape on the concrete floor, the jangle of chain between my ankles.

Of all the prize fixes a man can get himself into...

Ellis P. York. Private Investigator. Veteran. Some mother's son. And now: Enemy of the State.

And there...

In the barest of bare rooms, hunkered under a big round clock with hands in a race toward midnight, it waits—the electric chair.

It waits—rough-hewn, black, obscenely greasy-looking, as if lacquered with the rendered oils of each man it had embraced, bristling with buckles, manacles, and straps, all looking empty and hungry, like the chair itself, gaping for a victim to satisfy its grim appetite.

But it's the clock. It's the clock that fixes my eye. The sweeping, spider-like second hand, the big, marching minute hand, and the hour hand, thrust straight up like a dagger.

Thirteen minutes to midnight.

For a moment, the guards look at me—rigid, my head cocked back, staring—as if they think my nerve—or my mind—has deserted me. A profound pause—each molecule in the room frozen, like a pinball, poised at the zenith of its arc, before it pivots and sails downward, bouncing from rail to bumper to bell in its unpredictable course.

But my course has run out, and the end is as predictable as Thanksgiving turkey.

The guards, blinking dumbly, snap out of their moment's reverie. A nudge moves me forward. The shackles come off. Then, gently as you please, they show me to my seat.

A strap grips my right wrist, my left, both legs, then the big one around the chest. I feel my right pants leg being rolled up, something cold and jelly-like slathered on my shin, the sharp touch of metal. A priest, holding a Bible, mouths words I can't make out, but the tone, droning and hollow, is familiar.

I feel more eyes, now behind a darkened plate of glass, hiding behind the ghostly reflection of myself, like an image on a movie screen that stares back at me. And shining roundly above my head, forming, not a halo, but an evil moon, is the clock.

My mind buzzes with haunted flashes of thought and jigsaw pieces of incoherent memory. Every piece I try to fit together only makes more pieces, more questions. What did I do? How did I get here? Was it fate? Heredity? God's private joke? I keep running it through my brain, but something's screwy.

More goo, this time on my temples. An ill-fitting metal cap is fixed to my head. Reflected in the glass, the clock waxes full.

Shakespeare called death the sleep to end a thousand natural shocks. But only a few ticks of the clock separate me from the most unnatural shock of all.

Somebody asks me if I have any last words. For once—forever—I'm speechless. They don't ask a second time, and the world goes dark behind a black, canvas hood.

-2-

As usual, it all started with a dame...

I was at my office, somewhere on the downward slope of Hollywood. The ritzy nightclub across the street was a burlesque house now, its "Live Girls" sign flickering like a butt in a drunk's cupped hand. The old movie palace next door hadn't gotten the word about Technicolor. Tonight it was *Movie Crazy*, an old thigh-slapper starring Harold Lloyd. Tomorrow it would be some other forgotten flick usually found only in the back numbers of *Variety*.

I stood at the open window, dragging on a Chesterfield, my preferred brand, taking in the air coughed up by the beetle-backed cars that slithered like an endless centipede up Gower St. The Santa Anas were kicking up—first, a hot, dry whisper in my ear, then a gust that blew out the "S" on the "Live Girls" sign like a candle.

It was a lousy night in a string of lousy nights. The kind of night when you look at the lip of a bottle and the barrel of a gun and wonder which would taste better. On my desk, the bottle of Jim Beam was half empty. The army issue Colt was fully loaded. The devil on my shoulder made a strong argument, but the angel in my hand was more seductive. I filled it with another shot of rye.

I offered a toast to nothing as a shadow fell across my office door, where "Ellis P. York, Private Investigator," was spelled in reverse across the glass. The latch clicked. Instinctively, I grabbed the .45 and stepped back into the shadow.

The door cracked open and light spilled in over a permanent wave in shoulder pads and pumps. She stood there, poised with every curve in perfect silhouette, the kind of image you usually get in Hollywood only with Marlene Dietrich, a Kraut director, and a hundred grand in Klieg lights.

I liked the shape. I liked the shape just fine, but I wondered how the rest of the package looked.

"Hello? Is anyone there?"

No cigarettes and sauerkraut in that voice. It was pure California sunshine, with just the barest hint of L.A. smog.

I stuffed the .45 in the small of my back under my belt, eased one hand up the gooseneck lamp standing next to me, and snapped on the switch.

The light hit her full in the face. She let out a single breathy note of surprise, but didn't throw her hands before her eyes the way you might expect, just turned her face a few degrees and squinted into the light, as if she was trying to make me out. I don't know what she could see, but what I saw was a bit of all right: five-three, the comfortable side of a hundred and ten, dark eyes under frank, charcoal eyebrows, full, wide lips, and waves of midnight hair that showed auburn in the highlights. Somewhere between the girl next door and the girl next door's naughty cousin. But just my luck. A kid—nineteen, twenty at the oldest.

"Haven't you heard?" I barked, a little louder than I intended. "Lights out means nobody's home."

"You startled me," she said, as familiar as if she knew me.

"I'm not the one sneaking in on people."

She looked at the whiskey bottle on the desk—rather pointedly, I thought. "This is a place of business, isn't it?"

Cute, that. I liked her style, but in my office it's my show, so I unsheathed the .45— with a flourish more calculated than casual— slid open a desk drawer, and dropped the weapon in with a thud. At the sight of the cannon, her wide eyes went wider.

"Sure, it's a place of business—during business hours."

I slid open another drawer, pulled out a companion for my glass, and poured two stiff shots.

"Join me?"

"I didn't come here to drink."

My rule is what comes out of the bottle stays out of the bottle. I shrugged, poured her shot into mine, and downed it.

"I trust that hit the spot," she said.

"A near miss. That's as close as I ever get."

The barest snort. And not a snort that's really a laugh, but a snort that's really a snort. And in case I was too dense to get it, the look she gave me filled in the blanks.

Normally, a strange dame comes into my office and starts making with the holier-than-thou, I'd get sore, but there was something about this one. She was what guys in my racket commonly refer to as a "cute kid"—the kind of girl who hasn't yet become that kind of woman. If she'd been a blonde she'd be the young schoolmarm who used to make you want to recite your times tables just to see her smile. But she was no blonde, and I was no schoolboy.

I fished out another Chesterfield, tamped it, stuck it between my lips, and lit up as I rolled the words out of the side of my mouth.

"So whaddya want?"

"I need help."

"The YWCA is down the street."

Another look. Maybe anger, maybe something else. "I didn't come here to be insulted, either."

I sat down, stuck out my lower lip, and huffed a blue geyser toward the ceiling. "Okay, you didn't come here to drink, and you didn't come here to be insulted. So, why did you come here?"

She seemed to count to ten, glanced at the chair opposite me. "If you'll offer me a seat, I'll be happy to tell you."

"And if I don't offer, will you be just as happy to leave?"

She didn't make it past three, this time. She sat. It looked like I was going to get her spiel whether I liked it or not.

"It's your nickel."

She put a pink-palmed hand before her eyes. "Will you please get that light out of my face?"

"Sorry." I turned the gooseneck down toward the floor, and her eyes became two dark wells with the barest ripple of reflected light.

"Thank you."

She paused. I waited. Even in the half-dark I could read the uneasiness in her face.

"My name's...Vergos. Hellen Vergos. With two L's."

She spoke the name with emphasis, her look penetrating, as if she was watching to gauge my response.

"Okay," I said. "Mine's York. Ellis P. Also with two L's. Now what?"

But instead of answering, she just kept staring at me, waiting for something.

"Lady, either I'm hard of hearing or you're hard of speaking, because I'm not getting anything."

"I'm looking for someone."

"Good. Who?"

Another beat. She fumbled in her purse, fished out a photo. "A very dear friend. Here's his picture."

She handed it across the desk. I could feel her eyes measuring me as I looked at it: some round-spectacled swell, late twenties, maybe thirty, with slicked-back hair and a pencil mustache.

"How long has he been missing?"

"That's...hard to say."

Now it was my turn to look. "And why is that?"

Instead of answering, she shifted in her seat. "It's so dark in here. Can't we have more light?"

"I see fine. Has this dear friend got a name?"

"On the back."

I flipped the photo over, read aloud the name written there in a precise, practiced script: "'Hamlet Huffington Ravenswood III.' Is that a joke?"

She stiffened. "I assure you it is not."

"Maybe he's not missing. With a handle like that it could be suicide."

The look I expected, but the words surprised me.

"You didn't used to be so cruel."

I paused over a drag of nicotine to take close inventory of her features. Nothing.

"You don't say," I said. "Do we know each other?"

"We used to play together as kids. Don't you remember?"

She leaned forward, as if to give me a better look in the dim light. Still nothing. I tried the photo again.

"And this Huffington Puffington—did I play with him too?"

6

She looked at me for one miserable instant, then put her face in her hands and buckled over her knees. I poured myself another drink and let her work it out for herself. Autumn cloudbursts in L.A. rarely last long, and this one didn't either.

When she'd straightened up, her cheeks wet and shining in the lamplight, I said, "So you love this guy, huh?"

"Yes. I can't help it."

"Why should you help it?"

"Let's just say certain people don't approve."

She fumbled again in her purse, my deductive powers telling me for a handkerchief. And then it hit me. Why at that moment, I don't know, but I suddenly saw her very clearly in another time and place, as if the walls around me had given way to a long-forgotten tenement near Chinatown, her lipstick and permanent wave turned to cherry licorice and pigtails.

"Smelly Elly Vergos."

She practically levitated with joy. "You *do* remember!"

Images came to me: A narrow, cobblestone street, clamoring with brown immigrant kids; a squat, hairy man who drove a mule-drawn wagon every day to market.

"The fishmonger's daughter with Rockefeller dreams. All the neighborhood kids said you were stuck up."

She smiled as if at a compliment. "Your mother said I had dollar signs for eyes."

My mother was, shall we say, a sore spot with me. I could feel my lips twist into a grim non-smile. "My mother would know."

"You shouldn't say that. You don't know what your mother went through."

"That's right. She never stuck around long enough to tell me."

If she had information to enlighten me on the subject, she didn't share it. Instead, she sniffled and went back to the purse. I pulled a handkerchief from my pocket and tossed it to her.

"Here. Towel yourself down."

I watched her dab her eyes, took a long drag on my Chesterfield, held it as I snuffed the butt in an ashtray, then filled the air between us with blue haze.

She swatted at an imaginary mosquito. "You smoke too much." The schoolmarm again.

"A little habit I picked up during the war, courtesy of Uncle Sam. You want to complain, write your congressman."

I liked that one, decided to celebrate by pouring another drink.

"You drink too much, too."

"I also have a deviated septum, and I'm told that I snore." I raised my glass. "Cheers."

"Why do you work so hard at being horrible?"

"To protect the hurt, frightened, little boy that lives deep inside me?"

She held my gaze, nodding gravely, as if she were seriously considering my answer. I downed the drink, but it felt sour in my stomach.

Finished with the handkerchief, she held it out to me. "Thanks."

"Keep it." I tapped the photo to get us back on topic. "Have you filed a missing person report?"

"I can't. I'm not...family."

"So, has the family filed one?"

"You'd have to ask them."

She fished a card out of her purse, this time without the fumbling, and handed it to me.

"That's the address."

It was an embossed business card of a certain Colonel H.H. Ravenswood II, Ret. Brentwood address. Very ritzy.

"Talk to the Colonel first," Hellen Vergos was saying. "Mr. Ravenswood's father."

"*Mister* Ravenswood? Pretty formal for a guy you're supposedly in love with."

She blushed. Adorable. But the sight of her, those big, dark eyes dropping demurely to her lap, kicked up something inside of me, like dust in the moonlight.

Looking at her maybe a little too hard, I said, "I seem to remember, once upon a time, that you were sweet on me, too."

"What of it," she shot back.

I was surprised at the quick come-back. "Oh, nothing. It's just—"

"You teased me then, too, but you took up for me with the other kids. You were older. Wiser. A man of the world."

"You left out good-looking." I winked at her over my glass.

"You smoked and drank, even then." She flashed a smile, but it faded quickly. "Anyway, it was a long time ago."

Indeed it was. And I remembered something else, but I didn't mention it. The feeling had been mutual. Like she said, I was older, and when you're a kid, even a couple of years makes a big difference. Besides, she was like a little sister to me, and every time I caught myself looking at her out of the corner of my eye—at those cherry-licorice lips, at those long, brown legs—I wanted to give myself the same beating I'd give any other kid who looked at her sideways. By the time I realized she felt the same way about me, a third party came between us—Tojo, and that little shindig in the Pacific.

"You were saying?" I said. She looked blankly at me. "About the Colonel."

"Oh. The Colonel is old and in poor health. He doesn't take many visitors, these days, but he'll see you."

"How can you be so sure?"

She passed on that one. "It's probably a waste of time talking to his wife. Inez. If she knows anything she won't talk to you, and if she talks to you, she'll only tell you lies."

"Don't they all," I said. Looking right at her, but she didn't take the bait.

"If you learn anything, I can be reached at the Denmark Arms. On Larchmont."

She stood, ready to leave, but the meeting wasn't over as far as I was concerned. I tossed the card she gave me on the desk and held up a hand, traffic-cop style.

"Hold on, sister. Maybe you didn't get it when you read my name on the door, but that 'P' between the Ellis and the York stands for 'Poor.' All once-upon-a-times aside, I don't work for nothing."

She stiffened a little but apparently saw the justice of my plea. "Of course." Back to the purse, counted out a stack of five crisp bills, dropped them on my desk. "Is a hundred dollars enough?"

My impulse was to pounce on the cash like a junkie on smack, but I resisted it.

"It's a start."

Before I let her go I got a few more details on Ravenswood, but only a few. Whatever was going on, I was getting maybe half of it. A cagey client like that—especially one who thinks she can trade on past affections—usually spells trouble. But you can buy off a lot of trouble for a hundred in cold cash.

After showing Miss Hellen Vergos to the elevator—chivalry is part of the service—I returned to the five portraits of Andy Jackson where I had so coolly let them lie and scooped them into my hot, loving hands. We were going to be good friends, the five Andies and me, and the sweet music I imagined we'd make together drowned out the distant alarm bells that were going off in my head.

But what happened next was a regular klaxon.

The phone on my desk jangled. I picked it up and grunted, "York."

A husky male voice hissed over the line, "Don't trust her."

Something cold gripped me by the back of the neck, but I managed to growl, "Who is this?" The only answer was a click in my ear. I clacked the switch hook a couple times, saying, "Hello? Hello?" Dead air became dial tone, and I hung up.

I eyed the phone where it lay on my desk like a dead cat some neighborhood kid had left as a prank. When it became obvious the beast wasn't going to stir again, I lit up another cigarette, snapped off the gooseneck lamp, and sat back in my chair. An image came to me of the five Andies tucked away in my breast pocket having a good chuckle. I swiveled the chair around to face the window and watched the "Live Girl-" sign flash red in not-so-subtle warning.

-3-

I made it to the office the next morning at the crack of nine-thirty-seven. Sam, the half-Indian, half-Chinese, half-Mexican janitor greeted me with a folded *Los Angeles Times*, which I unfolded to find five little Lincolns snuggled inside.

Sam winked at me. "Told you that number was a winner!"

I didn't mention that he told me the same thing every week, usually with different results. "So you did, Sam. Tell you what." I slipped the paper back to him. "I'm feeling lucky. Why don't you put that on another winner. Keep five for yourself."

Sam looked at me like I'd just claimed to be Czar Nicholas, but he tucked the money away quickly enough.

"You betcha, Mr. York. Anything you say."

"Thanks, Sam."

"Thank *you*, Mr. York!"

Once I was back in the dingy confines of my cramped office, I was feeling a little less like Daddy Warbucks and more like the impoverished private dick I was. The morning sunlight angling through the blinds showed the layer of dust that covered every surface like a three-day stubble. I flicked on the overhead light, which helped with the dust but only highlighted the smudged walls and brown, water-stained ceiling.

My inner scold quipped, *No wonder you drink.*

The mail hadn't come yet, and Hellen Vergos' hundred dollars still warmed my heart enough that I skipped the bottle and went straight to work. Other people's money often had that effect on me. Especially when it came in the form of fresh, crisp bills that some working Joe or Jane had withdrawn from a sad, little savings account that was ever bobbing below the three-figure mark. That's how I saw Hellen Vergos: a weak swimmer who'd strayed from shore, trying not to flail her arms too obviously as her feet desperately reached for bottom. Cue my inner Boy Scout. Every little old lady on a street corner, every cat in a tree, every hard-working gal with a sob story had the intrepid Ellis P. York, Private Investigator Extraordinaire, as their champion. At least until lunch time.

A smart private investigator always goes through official channels on a case that might have police involvement, so I phoned a friend at Rampart Division. He was an affable sort, and we'd toured some of the same Pacific island paradises during the war, so he didn't mind helping me out from time to time when I had a missing person case. But it was no dice. It looked like Huffington Puffington—if he really was missing—wasn't official yet.

I was curious what kind of family didn't file a missing person report when they were missing a person, but the rich, as they say, are different from us. A visit seemed in order. The usual thing would have been to call first—the polite thing, so my mother once told me—but I was intrigued by Hellen Vergos' assurance that Col. Ravenswood would be delighted to have me drop by, so that's just what I decided to do.

***

Los Angeles, California, is the best city in the world for a drive. All those far-flung places, those wide, palm-lined boulevards in the flats, those winding, manzanita-skirted lanes in the hills. Sometimes I'll get on one of the main drags—Sunset, Sepulveda, Figueroa—and just drive, just to see how far it will take me.

My favored ride is a 1947 Packard Clipper 8, one of the first models off the line after they'd retooled from making engines for Uncle Sam's P-51 Mustangs. I'd wanted to "Skipper the Clipper," as the ads say, since I was a kid, and an honorable discharge with three years of combat pay was just the ticket to make it happen. I bought the first one I laid eyes on. It had the deep, "Packard Blue" lacquer finish, the two-tone English broadcloth interior, and a radio that could pick up the Rose Bowl broadcast all the way to San Pedro.

12

As a detective, the Packard was more than a car to me—it was a key part of the operation. It was a trademark, an office, a conference room, a shelter in bad weather, a life preserver in bad situations, a reliable flop, and, at the moment, even a restaurant. Having skipped breakfast, I stopped at a deli and picked up a corned beef on rye and a Dr. Brown's. With the sandwich in my hand and the soda bottle between my knees, I guided the Packard up Gower to Sunset, turned west, clicked on KFVD for a little jazz, and settled in for the long, lazy drive to Brentwood.

I'd finished my lunch and was enjoying a Chesterfield for dessert when I rolled past the Ravenswood place, giving it the once-over before I U-turned and approached the entrance.

It was one of those quaint, little Brentwood cottages, with what I judged to be about thirty-five rooms, done up in Tudor style, all medieval turrets and English ivy, but surrounded by acres of palm trees and tropical flowers. The kind of place where you have to make an appointment just to deliver the milk.

But when I pulled up at the gate, a guard emerged from his own little turret and waved me through as if I was the pool boy on the occasion of a major algae outbreak. I saluted him and glided on past.

The guard must have called ahead, because when I pulled up in the circular drive in front of the house a valet approached, smiling like he'd been waiting his whole life for the opportunity to open my door.

"Good morning, sir," he said, in a light, British lilt.

"Morning," I replied, getting out and pulling on my hat. "My name's York—"

"Yes, sir. The Colonel is waiting for you in the greenhouse. This way, sir."

The valet didn't say why the Colonel was waiting for me, or why he was in the greenhouse, and I didn't ask. My motto is, when expected, be expectable.

After fifty yards of listening to the valet's heels click smartly on the paving stones, and with no end of the house in sight, I had to ask, "Can we walk from here, or do we take the train?"

"It's not much farther, sir."

We rounded a stone edifice that would have done a Spanish fortress proud, and the greenhouse came into view. It was big enough for a commercial nursery, two stories of glass and more wrought iron than I'd seen since a tour of the French Quarter. The path that led to it passed through a Japanese tea garden, complete with moon bridge and koi pond. To the right was an English lawn that led down to a long, Italianate swimming pool, flanked on either side by columns of Tuscan cypress. So much for consistency in architectural design. In the pool, someone was doing the backstroke.

"This way, sir."

I followed him over the moon bridge and watched the koi, looking like Dr. Frankenstein's idea of goldfish, rise to the surface and blow us bubble kisses from their gaping mouths. The valet led me to a small, unassuming door, which he opened and indicated I should enter.

"After you, sir."

I stepped inside and was wrapped in a blanket of hot, liquid air, thick with the sweet smell of tropical flowers. The place looked like the inside of a Tarzan movie.

"Straight ahead, sir. Just follow the path."

"Thanks," I said. I was about to ask for a machete, but he was gone.

I made my way past voluptuous ferns, spiky bird-of-paradise, rubber trees, bananas, plants with leaves big as elephant's ears, thick, ropy vines, and every kind and color of flower imaginable, some big as hubcaps, some tiny as china thimbles. I was startled to see one brilliant bloom rise up and take flight, but it turned out to be a parrot. Something else feathered and tropical, with a beak like a curved dagger, cawed at me from the top of a date palm. The hot, syrupy air, redolent with the musk of teeming life, was making me dizzy, and I'd started groping my way like Stanley lost in the Congo, when a rich, oak-aged baritone called out to me from amid the verdure.

"Over here, my boy."

Following the voice, I changed directions, re-crossing the tile path I'd somehow lost.

"Here!"

Emerging from the greenery like a sinner from the baptismal font, I came to a courtyard where a hawk-nosed old memory of a man sat in a wheelchair, his withered legs—even in this heat—warmed by a gold, woolen tartan, his aristocratic beak sniffing at a white lily.

"Colonel Ravenswood, I presume?"

His neck craned stiffly in its high, starched collar, his eyes quizzical, as if he had forgotten he had just called to me, but then full of the pleasure of recognition.

"Yes! Yes! Let me look at you, my boy."

He did so, as I tried not to pose. I could feel the sweat trickling down my back, forming an expanding pool at the belt line. My hat seemed to have sprung a leak. I took it off, trying not to be too obvious in using it to mop the gathering flood of my brow. My coat, which usually flapped around me like a pup tent, clung like a rubber suit.

"Do you find it hot?"

"Hot?"

"Yes, hot. You look hot."

Glancing down at my shirt, I saw a dark stain emerging from beneath my tie. "I hadn't noticed," I said.

"I keep it this way for the orchids." A vague wave of the hand indicated the flowers that surrounded us. "And for myself. It's a pitiable excuse for circulation I'm provided by these old veins of mine. The greenhouse is the only place I feel comfortable."

Still not posing, I mopped the back of my neck with my handkerchief as he continued to take me in.

"Fine, fine. You look like you can take care of yourself. Not like these pigeon-livered milksops."

The same vague wave of the hand. Was he still speaking of the flowers?

"Sit, sit."

He gestured toward a rattan chair and cocktail table that sat facing him. I sat rigidly, hat between my knees, keeping my sweat-soaked torso from contact with the back of the chair.

The old man nodded at me with fatherly satisfaction as a nurse entered carrying a silver tray, decanter, and glasses. She was a bombshell blonde, her nurse's whites stretching over her curves as if it were a striptease costume instead of a uniform. She placed the tray on the table beside me, the old man watching her bend over, also with satisfaction, but decidedly less than fatherly.

"Thank you, my dear. That will be all."

She smiled and took her leave, her retreating locomotion an image I shall always cherish.

"Nice, um, place you have here, Colonel."

Another vague wave of the hand. "An unweeded garden that goes to seed."

It sounded like a quote, but I couldn't place it. "Seems okay to me."

"You like orchids, then?"

"Never thought much about them," I said in all honesty. I gave a look around to show my scientific curiosity. A big, bushy specimen about four feet around caught my eye. I pointed behind him. "That one's kind of interesting."

He tried to crane his neck to see over his shoulder, but the old bones didn't want to cooperate, and he had to wheel himself around, turning as slowly as a gun turret.

"Oh, that," he said at last. "You have an eye for the unusual, my boy. But that's no orchid. Come, have a look."

He wheeled himself closer, and I followed. Standing over the plant—or beside it, I should say, it was so big—it was obvious that it was different from the other flowers. Its leaves were lobed and heart-shaped, the size of candy trays, and it had strange pods, like elongated chili peppers tipped with big, curving hooks. The flowers were attractive enough, in the way so many tropical flowers are, halfway between beautiful and leprous. They were lavender to pink, trumpet-shaped at the stem, but flaring out into fat petals that formed a cross, or maybe a mouth, the swollen lips surrounding a diseased, yellow tongue at the center.

But the most unusual thing about the plant was that it seemed to be covered in some kind of thick, slimy dew that gave off a sickly smell, like fermenting potatoes.

16

"Pretty exotic," I said.

"Actually, it's the only native plant in my collection. *Proboscidea louisianica*, more commonly known as the devil's claw. It gets its name from the seed pods." With his finger he traced in the air the curve of the elongated tips. "When the pod drops off and the casing hardens, it splits, creating a two-pronged hook. The hook attaches to the hooves of grazing animals, often causing a wound. If the pod can't somehow be scraped loose, it remains embedded in the sore until the wound festers and the creature dies, the seeds germinating in the carcass."

I reached for a pod to have a closer look.

"Don't touch! Do you see the slime that covers the leaves and stems?"

"Yeah."

"It's a noxious substance, poisonous to small creatures. See the dead insects embedded in it? Food for the plant. It's a carnivore."

"Sort of a nasty thing to have around, isn't it?"

He started the slow process of returning his wheelchair to its former place.

"More so than you know. *Proboscidea* grow like weeds. If we didn't keep her pruned and burn all the seed pods she would take over the entire property."

He waved a hand and I took my seat.

"Why keep such a thing around?"

"She does have a certain beauty, don't you think? She caught your eye."

I noticed "it" had become a "she." "I suppose so."

"That combination of beauty and danger...That can be very attractive in a woman."

"Maybe. But we're talking about a plant."

"So we are."

There was an odd gleam in the old man's eye, and I began to wonder if he was quite right.

"Drink?" He indicated the decanter and glasses at my elbow.

"No, thanks," I said, my inner Boy Scout still on duty. "It's a little early in the morning for me."

"I happen to know that it is not," he said sternly. "Pour one."

In business, the customer is always right. I poured one glass half full, hovered the decanter over the second. "Are you joining me?"

"Never touch the stuff," he said wistfully. "Not any more. But I can watch you."

"To your health, then."

Ravenswood laughed. "To my health. That's rich."

I sampled the liquor. Good scotch.

"My compliments."

"Drink, drink."

I drank, his eyes drinking along with me.

"I knew you'd like it. Pour another."

It must have been my army training. I followed the Colonel's orders.

"You seem to know a lot about me."

"I make it my business to know about my business, young man. You're looking for my son."

"That's right. Have you missed him?"

"But he's not missing. He's only lost."

The second glass of scotch paused halfway to my lips.

"I'm afraid I don't take your meaning."

"You're 'afraid,'" the old man sneered. "That's a pigeon-livered phrase."

I shrugged. As long as the whiskey held out, he could say what he wanted.

"Who hired you?"

"I'm afr—That information is confidential."

"Ethical," he pronounced. "Living by the code of your profession, such as it is. Protecting your client. Good. I like that."

"I'm glad we understand each other."

"Oh, I understand you, all right. But do you understand? I want to know who hired you."

I put the glass aside. It looked empty and dejected next to the, as yet, undrained decanter. "I only have a couple of questions for you, sir. You can answer them if you like. Otherwise—"

"That girl."

"Beg pardon?"

"That Vergos girl. She hired you."

18

"If you say so."

He grunted. "Either you work cheap, or she's found some other way to pay you."

I felt my hands grip the arms of the chair, my legs tense to stand.

"I don't like that kind of talk."

That same hand-wave again. It was beginning to annoy me. "Never mind, never mind. I'm fond of the girl."

"I can tell."

"She used to work for me. Her mother, too."

"Is that right?"

He sighed. "So many used-to's. My life is positively filling up with used-to's."

"Beats the alternative, doesn't it?"

"Eh? Maybe, maybe..."

His mind seemed to drift a moment, then his eyes fixed on mine like a predator's.

"Why don't you come work for me?"

This conversation didn't seem to be getting me anywhere, but I played along.

"Mmm, I don't know," I drawled. "What did you have in mind?"

"You're good at finding things, yes?"

"I suppose so."

"That is your profession."

"Part of it. Yes."

"Good." He leaned forward, his eyes earnest. "You speak of my son. But I've lost something of *real* value."

He dangled the hook, but I wasn't ready to bite. Let him spill it.

He said: "My ram's horn."

I wanted to ask if he was kidding, but I could see he wasn't.

"Your ram's horn," I echoed. "Is that what you call it?"

"It's known as The Horn of Aries," he explained, oblivious to my crack. "A bejeweled sculpture of solid gold, crafted some four hundred years ago by artisans of the Caliph of Marrakech as a tribute to the Ottoman Emperor Suleiman the Magnificent."

He produced a slim volume from under the gold tartan, opened it where the page was marked, and showed me a photogravure of a gaudy, re-curved horn, crusted over with jewels, the exaggerated colors of the hand-painted plate giving it an unearthly vividness. Before I could read the caption the book snapped shut and retreated under the tartan like a rabbit down a hole.

"While in transit through the Straits of Messina—the treacherous waters of the legendary Scylla and Charybdis—the Barbary Corsair dispatched to deliver the gift was hit by a sudden storm and smashed to bits on the rocks. As the lifeless bodies of the ship's crew were still drifting in on the tide, the wreckage was picked over by Calabrian fishermen. The lucky fellow who recovered the Horn—on that very same night—got his throat slit for his trouble, and for four centuries since, that awful prize has been passed from hand to bloody hand—bargained for, fought for, killed for—with no one able to keep it who also wanted to keep his life. Some months ago, it came into my possession, but fell to the usual fate."

He leaned closer and whispered, "It was stolen from me."

"Yeah," I said. "I get it."

"Do you understand? My most prized possession. The very symbol of my wealth and power."

"Yeah?" Now it was my turn to give the wave of the hand. "So what do you call this mausoleum you live in?"

The Colonel sat back in his wheelchair, blinked twice, and chortled. "That's rich. Mausoleum. Yes. Yes, I suppose it is."

"That's quite a story, Colonel. How much of it is true?"

He shrugged. "All of it. None of it. What does it matter? I've seen the living article with my own eyes, held it in my own hands. You can't imagine how rare and beautiful a thing it is."

"And dangerous. Like your little flower."

He smiled, showing long, horse-like teeth. "You catch on. You asked a few moments ago why I kept my 'little flower,' as you call it. I wonder if you'll think me sentimental."

Not likely, I thought.

"It's a reminder. You see, *Proboscidea louisianica* has many names. Devil's claw. The unicorn plant. And...ram's horn."

"I see."

"The symbolism isn't too subtle, I trust."

"Subtle isn't the first word that comes to mind, no." I pulled out a pack of smokes. "Do you mind?"

"Another vice, another used-to that I once enjoyed. But you don't want that." He produced a carved box and lifted the lid on a handful of long, fat Cubans. "Have one of mine."

"Thanks." I selected one, sniffed it, and checked the label. "Romeo y Julieta," I said. "Isn't that the kind Churchill smokes?"

"Churchill never smoked one of these. Private stock."

I bit off the end and lit up, dragging heavily to get a good, even burn. The smoke was rich and thick as chocolate. It made my Chesterfields, by comparison, taste like hay.

"Not bad," I said.

"For what they cost, I hope they're better than not bad."

I shrugged, took another drag under his watchful, greedy eyes.

"So, this dingus of yours," I said. "How would I locate it?"

"Oh, that won't be any trouble. The, um, procurers have not found it so easy to dispose of their booty as they imagined. I'm arranging to buy it back."

"And you want me to go along and ride shotgun."

"If you're up to it."

"I'm up to it if the money is."

"Excellent."

Ravenswood pulled a checkbook and fountain pen from inside his jacket, scribbled out my name and a figure, tore off the check, and handed it to me.

The amount he'd written made my eyes cross: a cool thousand.

"There will be more, of course, when you finish the job. I'll contact you when the arrangements are made. It may be any time."

He held out his hand. I stood and took it—rather carelessly—my mind more on how quickly I could find a bank to cash that check. But he gripped my mitt in both fists and nearly pulled me down on top of himself. His eyes burned in their deep sockets as he held me. His words came out in a fierce, deliberate whisper.

"I find thee apt."

Off guard and off balance, I tried to brace myself against his chair, one foot doing stutter steps as the wheels backed away. "Howzzat?" I croaked.

"You're the only one I can trust in this matter," he said, his voice husky with feeling. "Prove to me that you are the man I take you for."

"Yes, sir," I said, affected. "I will."

I pulled my hand free and righted myself. The old man gazed up at me, his head bobbing like a vulture's.

It suddenly occurred to me that I was getting the bum's rush—although, considering the slip of paper in my pocket, it was a high-dollar bum's rush. I'd come here to get information on a missing person—a person who, theoretically, should have meant more to this old man than to me—and I had gotten almost exactly nothing. Despite the intensity of the Colonel's words, his attention was already back on his precious lily.

I put my hat on as if to go, stopped myself in mid-turn, and said, "Oh, one more thing, sir."

"Yes?"

"All fatherly concern aside—any idea where I might find your son?"

"Certainly. Just knock on any door of any speakeasy in town. You'll find him."

I nodded my thanks and left.

Back out on the lawn, I saw that the backstroker had left the pool and stretched out on a chaise longue. Even at this distance I could see she was a looker, lithe and lightly burnished by the sun, her hair in a rubber cap, her suit sticking out in all the right places. Even though her eyes were shielded behind dark glasses, it was obvious she caught sight of me, but she turned away as if I wasn't there.

But I was there, and if this was the wife Hellen Vergos had warned me about, I told myself, she could lie to me all day.

I took a step, and suddenly felt a firm hand planted on my shoulder. It was the valet.

"This way, sir," he said, pleasant as you please, indicating with his free hand the direction opposite where I was facing.

He was a slight fellow, a full head shorter than me, but his hand was as rigid against my shoulder as a Red Grange stiff-arm.

"I want to talk to the lady," I said.

"Sorry, sir. The Missus isn't taking visitors today."

I didn't mind the brush-off, but the strong-arm treatment rubbed me the wrong way.

"Move that hand, or I'll move it for you."

His smile was as placid as a buttered scone. "Let me show you to your car, sir."

I gripped him by the wrist. The next thing I knew, I was on my back, arms and legs in the air like a flipped crab.

"Sorry about that, sir. Let me help you up."

He pulled me to my feet. I hooked his forearm and spun around for my best judo flip, but he turned it back on me and sent me sprawling again.

"So sorry, sir. Shall I help you up again?"

"I'll manage, thanks." I got to my feet, dusted myself off with what dignity I could muster. As far as I could tell, the woman at the pool had missed the show.

"Where did you learn judo like that?"

"Her Majesty's Dragoons, sir. Six years in Burma, China, spots and places. You a veteran, sir?"

"Guadalcanal."

"Nasty bit of business, that. Your form's right enough. Just a bit rusty, I imagine."

"Thanks for the lesson."

"My pleasure, sir."

-4-

Safe again from mad dogs and Englishmen in the friendly confines of the Packard, I rolled back up Sunset, cut south on Sepulveda to Wilshire, and made like a homing pigeon for the First National Bank of Beverly Hills, a Romanesque temple to the Great God Commerce, where Colonel Ravenswood and other high priests of Southern California affluence worshipped.

I traded the check for a stack of playmates for the five Andies, fattening my wallet so that it weighed over my heart like an engorged tumor. The bare facts: Yesterday, I'd had no jobs and no prospects. Today, I had two jobs and eleven hundred bucks in my pocket. According to these facts, I should have been happy. But I maneuvered the Packard through Wilshire traffic as if every car and stoplight were a personal insult, brooded over the stub of the Romeo y Julieta that burned under my nose like the rank weed that it was. Something was rotten. Even over the cigar I could smell it.

Fortunately, detective work is the perfect complement to a foul mood. I pitched what was probably a dollar's worth of Cuban tobacco out the window and lit up one of my own. Despite the Colonel's flipness when I had asked about his son's whereabouts, I decided to take his answer as confirmation that Hamlet Huffington Ravenswood III was indeed missing, or at least had not been seen recently, by people who cared about him or otherwise.

So, I decided to check all the usual suspects in a missing person case: hospitals, drunk tanks, the morgue. On a wild hunch, I tried the drunk tanks first. Nobody had seen him lately, but I got some strange cracks about the photo that seemed to indicate he was an imbiber of some reputation. I struck out at the morgue, too, which I chalked up as good news to report. Using a pay phone on Alvarado as a temporary office, I called admissions at every hospital in the area. No Ravenswoods had been checked in anywhere—Huffington or otherwise—but two hospitals had John Does that fit the description. One was downtown, just a few blocks away, and the other was in Eagle Rock.

Neither lead panned out, and after a full day of flat-footing it, I was in bad need of a bath and a drink. I opted for the drink first. Heading back from Eagle Rock down Alameda, I spotted a storefront joint called Brownie's Grille and Bar, and despite that worrisome little "e" decided to give it a try.

The place was new to me, but it was familiar enough in type: a cramped, neighborhood joint that stank of day-old cigarettes and ethylized sweat. Several besotted regulars were in a clutch at one end of the bar, with the tonier clientele sprinkled around sad, rickety tables with matchbooks stuck under their uneven legs. Brownie—a rotund, wreath-haired, little fellow in a faded green apron—presided over the place with the good cheer of a man who never expected more out of life than was handed to him.

I dropped my hat on the bar and sidled onto a stool. Brownie asked me what I'd have, and I picked out a bottle of middle-grade bourbon and the least-dirty glass I could see. Brownie poured the first one. I raised the glass to his health and slid the elixir down, feeling it dissolve warmly into my gullet.

My mood improved substantially. The place was just about perfect: serviceable liquor, comfortable atmosphere, and an amiable, not-too-talkative proprietor. The only sour note was a particular item of décor, which was, in fact, the commonest and sorriest fixture a drinking man could ever hope to see staring back at him from behind the rows of delightful glasses and booze. Namely—a mirror. That silent, needling, little friend that mouths every word you speak and mocks every move you make, ever-ready, if you dare utter any reproach, to throw your face right back in your face. The swank places all had them, which was one reason I usually preferred the dives.

But I got over it. Did I mention the serviceable liquor?

Still, something was nagging at me. I couldn't get the old man out of my head. Frail and thin-blooded as that old hothouse orchid was, he had a grip like iron and eyes as burning and predatory as a cougar's. Twenty minutes I'd sat in his private *Bomba, the Jungle Boy* movie set, sweating like a pig on a spit, first getting a botany lesson, then a cockamamie story about pirates and sultans and lost treasure, but not one straight answer to a single question I had come to ask. True, I turned a quick thousand dollar profit for my troubles, but that was clearly a payoff, one I was apparently neither too proud nor too ethical to accept. I didn't doubt he had some sort of little job for me to do, and I'd do it, but whether I'd lay off of trying to find his son was another story. That is, assuming laying off was what he wanted. I wasn't so sure, since he struck me as the kind of man in the habit of spelling out very plainly any specific demands he might have. Was he trying to buy my loyalty, in case I turned up something nasty on Junior? Then why the flip attitude about his disappearance? Why not try to win my sympathy with some good, old fatherly worry and grief? The one solid bit of information I did get was that Hellen Vergos had once worked for him—if "work" was the word. In any case, there was something between them. If I knew what that was about, maybe things would make more sense. Then there was that strange earnestness before we parted. Was it a con? Whatever the case—whether it was all real or just an elaborate bag of tricks—I'd been thrown off my stride. The old man had gotten under my skin, somehow, found a little chink in my normally bulletproof armor, and that bugged me. My assessment was that he was mean, callous, possibly dangerous, and definitely fond of shading the truth. Maybe that's why I liked him.

I'd just finished the third leg of a trifecta, when I decided to test the Colonel's theory about his son being just a knock away. I called for Brownie, who, being a man of good business sense, was swiftly there with merchandise in hand.

"Another?"

"Good question," I observed, my manner become expansive. "Three men on. Who's batting cleanup?"

Brownie got it. He turned the label up and said, "Looks like George Dickel."

"Let's see what he's got."

As Brownie poured, I pulled out the photo I'd gotten from Hellen Vergos and showed it to him.

"Ever see this guy in here?"

Brownie took the photo, glanced at it, turned on me a suddenly suspicious eye.

"What's the racket?"

"Whaddya think? I'm a private investigator. Junior's gone missing from the family homestead."

Brownie smiled with practiced good nature.

"I get it." He studied the photo very seriously and very seriously shook his head. "Nope. Never seen him before."

He handed the photo back to me with a sly wink. I didn't like it.

"You getting smart with me?"

I could feel some of the regulars' ears pricking up, saw in the mirror several heads swivel in my direction.

He shook his head with exaggerated slowness. "N-o-o-o-o, I wouldn't think of it."

He winked again, then a jolly look around, as if everybody was in on the joke.

Over Brownie's shoulder I saw my reflection give a distasteful leer and toss a fiver onto the bar top.

"You need to stop sampling the merchandise."

I grabbed my hat and shoved my way out the door, trailing a gaggle of muttering voices behind me.

-5-

The liquor at Brownie's was fine, but the bartender left a bad taste in my mouth. Outside, the air was cool, the sky a deep turquoise with streaks of red along the hills. Streetlights flickered on up and down the boulevard. I checked my pocket watch. If I headed back to the office now I'd be there by quitting time. Perfect.

As I got off the elevator I saw an elegant, leggy blonde, thirty-fivish, in a red-and-black "business" ensemble that cost three hundred dollars if it cost a nickel. On her head was the kind of architecturally improbable structure that wouldn't normally pass for a hat unless Joan Crawford was sitting under it. She was standing at my office door, smirking at my name on the glass, her expression somewhere between complete disdain and utter indifference.

I didn't much like the way she looked at my name, but I liked everything else about her just fine. A real package. A real *expensive* package. The French have a phrase for a woman like that. But my French was rusty, so it came out an all-American wolf-whistle.

She turned, her head tilted back so that her crystal-blue eyes seemed to look down at me from under smoky, thick-lashed lids. A listless wave of a gloved hand indicated my name.

"This is you, I suppose." Her voice was cultured—practiced, maybe—but dark as ashes in bourbon.

"You suppose right."

"Clever boy. May we go in?"

I approached the door, forced to crab-walk past her when she didn't step aside. I clicked the latch with my key and pushed the door open.

"After you."

She entered, standing just inside as I flicked on the light. With one sweep of her eyes, she took it all in. If the seaminess of the place disgusted her, she was too bored to show it.

She didn't seem to have the knack for giving ground, so I had to brush past her to pull out a chair. Apparently, the proximity was a little too much, because she made a face.

"You reek of whiskey."

"It's casino night at the CYO. Those nuns get pretty wild."

Her not-so-polite smile showed what she thought of my humor. She eyed the grimy seat of the chair I held for her for one dubious second, then sat.

That's when I noticed the pin on her lapel—a jeweled, cornucopia-like horn, the size of a two-bit piece, a miniature of that depicted in the Colonel's book.

I made my way around to my side of the desk, pulled the Jim Beam out of the drawer.

"Drink?"

Her expression said no. I shrugged and put the liquor away.

She said, "I saw you at the house today."

"The house?" Then it hit me. "Oh, you mean the mausoleum."

"You might have noticed me by the pool."

"I might've. You're Inez Ravenswood."

"Well, you *are* a detective."

"Hellen Vergos told me about you."

"I'm sure she did. Did you find what you were looking for?"

"Looking for?"

"In the greenhouse."

I shrugged. "Not exactly."

"Hm. I'd heard you'd come to ask about Hammie. Imagine my surprise—"

"Hammie?"

"Hamlet Huffington Ravenswood III. My stepson."

"Of course."

"Why, what should we call him?"

I passed on that one and made a prompting gesture. "Imagine your surprise..."

"When you didn't come to see me."

I let my eyes slide down the pearly curve of her neck to the various parabolas of her figure in a way I intended as frankly appraising. "Yeah, I'm a little surprised myself. On the other hand, that Limey valet of yours wasn't too keen on letting me disturb your swim."

"Jeffers? Surely he's harmless."

I didn't argue. She pulled a silver cigarette case from her handbag, clicked it open, and selected a long, French blend for which she waited vainly for a light. She was game, though. She didn't produce one of her own and she didn't ask, and if my incivility irritated her, you'd have never known it from the expression of placid boredom on her face. Finally, I tapped out one of my own and lit us both up.

"Thank you so much."

"So," I said. "Let's say I had come talk to you. What would you have told me about little Hammie?"

"It depends. What exactly would you like to know about him?"

"Let's start with when was the last time you saw him."

"That also depends."

"On what?"

"On whether you mean the last time I saw him, the last time I spoke to him, or the last time I knew where he was."

"Okay-y-y, let's start with the last time you saw him and break it down from there."

She extruded a long, lazy stream of perfumed smoke that folded on itself in the air like ribbon candy. "This must be a dull business. Do you always deal in such trivialities?"

I blew an ak-ak burst of my own that knocked a round hole right through her ribbons. "Why don't you let me decide what's trivial?"

"It won't do you much good to know where Hammie was a week ago or even a day ago. What you want to know is where he might turn up next."

"And how would I find that out?"

"Oh, by studying his habits, getting into his psyche, observing the subject in his un-natural environment. Think of it as a psychological excavation."

30

She seemed to be enjoying herself now, her cold smirk taking on a whimsical quality that only gave it a crueler turn.

"Sounds very scientific, but I don't go in for the Sherlock Holmes stuff."

"I was thinking more Dr. Freud."

"I don't go much for him, either."

"So what do you go for?" Crossing her long legs.

Now it was my turn to smirk.

"Don't get ahead of yourself, big boy."

"Oh? Am I going too fast, Officer?"

She snorted a blue stream. "You don't have the horsepower."

"That tears it. Let's get back to your stepson."

She frowned. "'Stepson.' That makes me sound like such a matron."

My eyes couldn't help glancing back at those legs. "I wouldn't worry about it. Nobody's mistaking you for Ma Kettle."

The dead pan again. "Nobody'd be wise not to."

It was going to take me a minute to get my head around that one. I took another tack. "So what else can you tell me about Hammie? You know, what kind of guy he is, who his friends are. . ."

"Hammie is a confused, pampered young man with the interests of a child and the bad habits of an old man."

As answers go, it wasn't too heavy on facts, but it was straight enough.

"What sort of interests?"

A pause, amused eyes gauging me. "He likes playing cops and robbers."

"Meaning he's interested in the law, or in trouble with it?"

"Both."

"Okay. And the habits?"

"Drink, mostly."

"Women?"

A forced smile. "He fancies himself a one-woman man."

"Hellen Vergos."

"For the moment. I suppose she's had you looking simply everywhere for him."

"Not everywhere," I said, getting fed up with her perfumed cigarette and her self-satisfied air. I set my eyes on a spot eight inches above her head. "I haven't looked under that hat."

She colored. *Touché!*

"What exactly brings you here, Mrs. Ravenswood?"

"In keeping with your droll wit, I suppose I should say my limousine. But what I *want*, Mr. York, is for you to drop this whole ridiculous charade."

"And I suppose you're prepared to pay me handsomely to do so."

She stood. "On the contrary. I'm prepared to pay you exactly nothing."

I got up and eased around the desk.

"Then you're asking me as a personal favor."

"Something like that."

I stood close to her. "But I only do favors for friends."

"You'll find I can be very friendly. Under the right circumstances."

"How friendly?"

I moved closer. When she didn't retreat, I leaned in and kissed her, full on her red lips. It wasn't quite like kissing a lamppost, but that wasn't the point. The point was the look on her face when I pulled back. Or what I thought her look would be. Surprisingly, her expression was as unsmudged as her lipstick, but I knew she was sore. I stuck out my grinning mug and pointed at my chin.

"Go ahead. Let me have it."

Boy, did she. She was on me like a vampire on blood, with a ten thousand volt kiss that buckled my knees.

When she released me, her face was all cold triumph and I was gasping for air.

"I'll be at the Club Blue Angel at ten o'clock. Do come."

There was a ringing in my ears, and the next thing I knew, she was out the door.

"Hey, wait a minute—"

The ringing turned out to be the telephone.

"Hey!" I started to go after her, but she was already at the elevator and the phone wouldn't shut up.

I went back to my desk and picked up. "York."

That same husky voice came hissing over the line.

"You're getting in over your head, York."

"Who is this? What do you want?"

"I want what you want, York."

My head was spinning for real now, my voice at a heightened pitch. "Ravenswood? You're looking for Ravenswood?"

Laughter rattled in my ears, then cut out as the line went dead. I shouted at the phone like a madman. "Who is this! What do you want!"

And then I heard ringing again. And the voice. It said, "Pick up the phone, dummy."

I grunted a question, my tongue suddenly thick in my mouth, and looked down at the phone.

Nausea rippled through me. A trickle of cold sweat oozed from my scalp. The phone's receiver was back in its place, the hand that had held it only a moment ago empty. I stared at my naked palm, stared at the malevolent beast that cried shrilly on my desk. For a fleeting instant I thought Inez Ravenswood must have slipped me a mickie—but no, her kiss may have been poison, but not in that literal sense. It was just one of those dizzy spells I'd had since the war. So they'd gotten worse. Nothing to get hysterical about.

What I needed was a drink. Or maybe not. The empty bottle was lolling on my desk next to an empty glass.

Swallowing against the dryness in my throat, I picked up the phone and lifted it to my ear, listening before I spoke. When I got only silence I said, "What do you want?"

"Hello? Mr. York? Is this Ellis York?"

A different voice.

"Yeah, this is York. Who's this?"

"This is Ravenswood. Are you all right, my boy?"

"Col. Ravenswood." I tried not to sound relieved. "Yes, I'm fine, sir. What can I do for you?"

"Things have moved rather quickly since we spoke this morning. It's all set."

"The payoff?" My head felt like it was full of cotton, but the coincidental timing of his call managed to seep through.

"Yes, for the dingus, as you call it. My lawyer, Fred Fergus, is handling the transaction. Meet him at the corner of Mulholland and Laurel Canyon tonight at midnight. He'll have the money, and your instructions. Can I depend on you, son?"

"Absolutely, sir. I'll be there."

"It will be well worth it to you."

"Yes, sir. Thank you. Ah, Col. Ravenswood—?"

The line clicked.

"Hello?"

He was gone. Just as well. I had no idea what it was I'd wanted to ask him.

I checked my watch and was surprised to see that it was already half-past eight. I seemed to have misplaced an hour somewhere. Still, plenty of time to get cleaned up and make it to the Club Blue Angel by ten o'clock. There was no telling what Inez Ravenswood was cooking up, and I wanted to be there when she dished it out.

Remembering why I had come back to the office in the first place, I deposited nine hundred and fifty of the thousand dollars Col. Ravenswood had given me in the little vault set into the floor under the trashcan. The other fifty I kept for my landlady. I stuffed the .45 in my shoulder holster, tugged my hat down over my eyes, and cut the light. Glancing out the window, I noticed that the movie marquee across the street had been changed. It read: *This Gun for Hire.*

-6-

My current legal residence was at the Elsinore Court Apartments on Sycamore, owned by a sweet, old broad by the name of Bailey, who'd made a little money in the silent days as one of Mack Sennett's original Bathing Beauties and been smart enough to invest in real estate. Now she was retired, living off the income provided by her "kids," as she called her tenants. Everybody called her "Ma," even the stooped, wispy-haired Japanese gardener, whom she seemed to be constantly haranguing to re-pot, re-plant, or re-arrange some bit of horticulture he had already re-worked a dozen times before, as if she were ever tweaking some grand, shapeless masterwork, the ideal form of which was only contained in her head. Although the gardener spent a suspicious amount of private time with her—taking daily teas, late-evening sherries, and even meals in her chambers—she could never seem to get his name exactly right, mangling it in a way we tenants always heard as "Mr. Tomahto."

I came up the walk, where she stood over the stooped man, expostulating on the incorrectness of the shade of purple displayed by a clutch of bougainvillea.

"Mr. Tomahto, I distinctly asked for mauve blooms. These are positively puce!"

Mr. Tomahto, who spoke perfectly clear English when he wanted to, responded with a stream of Japanese that seemed to express his own colorful ideas about the disposition of the bougainvillea.

"A little late in the evening for gardening, isn't it," I called, cordially tipping my hat.

"Oh, Mr. York," she said, as if she'd been expecting me. "Mr. Tomahto and I were just about to retire for a bit of sherry. Would you like to join us?"

I'd played that scene before. The sherry was bad enough, but she kept her apartment like a memorabilia-stuffed shrine to her former self, the beauty queen and promising Hollywood starlet. I found it depressing.

"Can't tonight, Ma. Got a hot date."

"Oh? Anyone I know?"

"Don't think so. She's a gypsy knife-thrower I met at the circus. Cute, but she doesn't have any arms. Throws with her toes."

She wagged a scolding finger at me. "One of these days I'm going to believe one of your tales."

I put my hand over my heart. "I only tell them to make you jealous."

She laughed in a girlish way that made the years seem to rest on her with soft pillows. I realized Mr. Tomahto must have thought she was a pretty sweet number.

"By the way," I said, "I've got a little something for you." I flashed the bills before her amazed eyes. "That should bring me up to date, plus two weeks in advance."

She thanked me and promised to leave a receipt in my mailbox. As I headed to my apartment I heard her whisper to Mr. Tomahto, "You see, I told you he was a good boy." Mr. Tomahto returned with a comment I couldn't make out. Maybe it was about the bougainvillea.

Ma had been offering for months to help me "decorate" my room, but so far I had resisted, partly out of fear that it would turn into another project, like the garden, that could outlive us all, and partly because I liked things the way they were. I had walls to keep out the weather, Venetian blinds to keep out the sun, a bed to sleep on, a sink to wash in, a chest of drawers to dress from, and a hot plate for coffee and the occasional fried egg. What more could a man want?

In so sparsely furnished a cell, one would think that a break-in would be easy to detect, that with so few objects in the room, the slightest displacement of any one would immediately show itself.

But I guess I was in a hurry, throwing off my sweat-stained clothes, splashing myself with soap and water, making myself look my best for the night ahead, whatever it may bring. It wasn't until I was sitting on the bed, giving my shoes a quick brush, that I noticed anything.

The bed was exactly where it always was, or close enough. What gave it away were the scuff marks, the two long streaks on the tile, like elongated commas, that showed where one end of the bed had been slid out about three feet and put back.

I felt that cold thing grip me by the back of the neck again, but I shook it off and gave the place a quick once-over. Nothing.

I pulled on my shirt and suspenders and went to Ma's apartment. Soft music was wafting out the window, stopping suddenly at the sound of my knock. When Ma answered the door, there was a single, long wisp of gray hair that stuck straight out from the side of her head, and although there were two glasses of sherry on the parlor table, Mr. Tomahto was nowhere in sight.

I asked her if anyone had been in my apartment, which she took immediate offense to. It took me a minute to explain that I had no suspicions about her—or anyone else, for that matter—but that it appeared someone had tried to break in—

"Break in!" she exclaimed. "You mean a burglar?"

And she would likely have had all of L.A.'s finest swarming over the place in minutes had I not been able to talk her down again. I've got no beef with the cops in general, but in particular it's a different story, and it's always a roll of the dice who, in particular, might show up for a call. Besides, I like to keep my business my business. Begging pardon for misspeaking, I explained to Ma that I had just been expecting someone and wondered if she'd noticed whether anyone had stopped by. I got the chary "no" I expected and went back to my room.

I sat on the bed, brooding over the scuff marks. More so than commas, they looked like the hooked prongs of the devil's claw. I got down on all fours, looked under the bed again. Nothing there. I pulled one end of the bed out from the wall, just as the intruder had done, about three feet into the middle of the floor. Nothing under it, nothing behind it.

And then I realized that it wasn't about what was under the bed, it was what was above it. The light fixture. I looked up, and there it was—a dark square of gray showing through the frosted glass dome.

I stood on the end of the bed and found myself perfectly positioned to reach up and retrieve the object. It was a square of paper, folded over. I opened it, once, twice.

On it was a crude, but not unskilled, ink rendering of a man pierced through the back with some kind of long spear, or lance, that dripped gobbets of ink-black blood. The drawing was detailed enough to include the man's fedora, coat, and tie, along with a convincing grimace of pain across his face. One interesting touch was that the man did not appear to be standing or falling, but rather suspended in air, arms and legs crooked before him, giving the impression of an insect, or maybe a voodoo doll, skewered on a pin.

I felt that dizziness again, and a sudden heat that made me break out in a sweat, but I was able to fight it, blinking and breathing deliberately as I focused on the image. There was no other message or distinguishing marks. It looked like little more than the ghoulish doodle of some teenage boy with too much imagination, but it held some significance that I couldn't get a handle on. If it was a threat, why hide it? Why so indirect? And if it was a curse—well, I wondered what kind of cut-rate voodoo witch I'd crossed that made do with a drawing of a doll instead of the real thing.

Not being the superstitious type, I refolded the drawing and tucked it in my wallet. The remaining Andies kept their counsel, watchful and mum around the new guy.

My watch said nine-forty. Time to get to the Club Blue Angel.

-7-

Despite the night's chill, I drove with the windows down, letting a cigarette dangle from my lip unlit so as to better savor the star-filtered air. The Club Blue Angel was a hot hangout where Hollywood swells could get their jollies mingling with real, live gangsters. According to the gossip rags, Bugsy Siegel used to have a regular table, back before he got clipped, and on any given night a lucky patron might find himself rubbing elbows with anyone from Hepburn and Tracy to Olsen and Johnson.

The place was owned by a Kraut by the name of Claude Geiger, who supposedly escaped from Germany just before the blitzkrieg. Rumor had it that he was a quack doctor who enjoyed considerable favor with the SS until he'd muffed an operation on the wrong Nazi. Like many an immigrant before him, he'd come to these shores with nothing but a dream, as naked of his past transgressions as a newborn babe. He'd had a skill to sell, though, and made a tidy little income in New York as a knife-for-hire doing back room surgery and face jobs for some unsavory characters—no questions asked and strictly cash. Like a lot of other talented Germans on the outs with Der Fuhrer, he'd eventually come to Hollywood, and through good old American pluck and hard work, not to mention mob connections, he'd remade himself into a successful businessman.

The joint was tucked away just off Sunset, but easy to spot all done up in "mood indigo" neon that reflected like phosphorous off the hood of the Packard. I pulled up behind a line of cars, and a parking valet in a red monkey suit opened my door and handed me a ticket. I tipped him a buck as insurance against any maltreatment of the Packard, and he thanked me enthusiastically in what sounded like Italian.

What is this, a halfway house for reformed fascists? I filed that one away for future investigation.

The doors of the club were two button-studded cushions of red leather, tinged garishly purple by the blue neon and looking like twin couches on brass hinges, something like the gates of Hell might look, if Satan were a nightclub owner. An easel to the side carried a placard depicting a Negro jazz singer, dramatically posed with a big blue flower in her hair, and emblazoned with the name "Dahlia!"

Two doormen, also dressed in red monkey suits, also tinged purple by the blue lights, opened the doors like figurines on a Black Forest clock. I clicked my heels, gave them my best Erich Von Stroheim bow, and entered.

The interior of the place looked like something from a Busby Berkeley fever dream—soaring, art deco colonnades, jeep-sized wall sconces that threw wedges of lurid blue light to the ceiling, full-grown potted palms that seemed to have wandered in from Beverly Hills, and scores of white-on-white cocktail tables with silver buckets of champagne being swilled by the Hollywood elite, the men in black tie, the women in diamonds and chintz. The bandstand was rimmed with the signature blue neon and seemed to float a foot above the dance floor on a cushion of swinging jazz provided by an enormous white-jacketed orchestra. Front and center, singing an up-tempo number with effortless grace, was Dahlia, light-skinned, late thirties, with fine features and wide, Egyptian eyes, elegant in a cascade of jewels and gold lamè, her namesake flower perched over one diamond-studded ear, like a halo that had been knocked askew.

I liked her sound, and stopped to listen, but the Maître D', a man so pink he looked like he'd been sand-papered, interrupted my listening with an ostentatious sniff.

"Have you a reservation, sir?"

He eyed my plain, gray suit like it was something I'd skinned myself.

"I'm meeting Mrs. Ravenswood," I said.

He gave me a skeptical look, but I weathered it. He checked his book, found her reservation, and graced me with a pinched, grudging smile.

"Mrs. Ravenswood hasn't arrived yet. Perhaps you'd care to wait at the bar?"

This guy could make "God bless you" sound like "Go to hell," but I let it pass.

Dahlia finished her number with a high, piercing note, and I stopped on my way over to the bar to join in the applause. She bowed, and then—as if she could distinguish my clap from the hundreds of others in the audience—looked right at me. For a moment, we locked eyes, but if she'd picked me out of the crowd it was probably only because I was conspicuous, standing there in my dull suit amongst the shiny, seated patrons. Her expression was enigmatic, distant, as if neither I nor the audience were really there, and she bowed again, in a way that seemed more out of habit than acknowledgment.

I found a seat at the end of the bar nearest the bandstand. The bar area was twice the size of Brownie's whole joint and had five times as many mirrors—mirrors on the walls, mirrors on the ceiling, even the bar top itself was one long mirror. Depending on which way you looked, you could see yourself in profile, from behind, or even upside down. Nice effect. If the liquor didn't make you dizzy, the décor would.

The orchestra changed the tempo with a few slow, moody chords, and I turned my back on the fun-house saloon to listen. The bartender sidled up to me with a "What'll ya have," and I did something that is normally against my policy—I waved him off. Dahlia was singing.

The song was "No Regrets," a favorite of mine since I'd heard Billie Holiday sing it with Duke Ellington at the Club Alabam, back when I was a kid playing escort for my mother on one of her late-night prowls. Not to take anything away from Lady Day, but Dahlia sang that song as if it had been written just for her—or maybe as if it had never been written at all, as if each note was the pure expression of her soul:

Loved the high life—
Low-lit places,
Brassy music,
Sassy faces...

And her soul did ache. You could see it in her shimmering eyes, hear it in her quavering voice. This woman had known pain, and she seemed determined to put the melody on the same rack that had tormented her, stretching whole phrases to the breaking point, lowering one note to a barely musical gasp, raising another to an ear-shattering wail.

Loved to gamble—
Place your bets—
Loved a man,
Mortal man...
No regrets...

Everything in the place—the mirrored bar, the lurid lights, the glittering swells—vanished, until I saw and heard nothing but Dahlia, vivid in a blue, baby spot. My heart seemed to slow to the beat of the song, my breathing to stop altogether. At one point even Dahlia melted away, leaving only her voice, which had a presence of its own, enveloping me like a succubus, spinning me round and round until I, too, had vanished.

I took aim for the heart—
Always aim for the heart...
Now he's gone,
No regrets...
Now I'm done,
No regrets...no regrets!

And then something jostled me, and there was a roaring in my ears. Images turned like a kaleidoscope before my eyes, and I was jostled again, fingers poking at my shoulder.

I heard applause, and a voice asking me a question.

The house lights were back up, my dazzled eyes blinking against them as Dahlia took her bows. The bartender said, "You all right, Mac?" his hand reaching again toward my shoulder.

"Stop poking me," I growled. "Can't you see I'm enjoying the show?" And I joined the audience with a few claps of my own just to show him.

"Sorry," he said. "I thought you might've needed some help."

"What I need is a bourbon. Neat." When he hesitated, I added, "Yeah, I'm sure."

He put his hands up defensively and got it.

I downed it as the orchestra kicked into a mid-tempo instrumental, a lolling respite from Dahlia's wrenching song.

I rapped my empty on the mirror, wondered why it didn't crack.

"Another."

The bartender obliged.

"Look, I didn't mean nothing a minute ago," he said. "It's just sometimes you—"

"I know, I know," I said. "You let a guy drink too much, people might get the idea they're in a bar."

He flushed. "Look, Mac, I was just trying to apologize."

I hate apologies, especially when they make me feel like a heel. He was a mop-topped redhead with a fat, cherubic face and wide, innocent eyes that looked back at me with childlike hurt.

"Forget it."

Then everything went gray for a second, and I must have teetered on the bar stool.

"You sure you're okay?"

This guy was in the wrong business. He should've been a nurse's aide.

"Just a little dizzy spell," I said, feeling exasperated, more with myself for telling than him for asking. "Had 'em since the war."

"You a vet?"

"Isn't everybody, these days?"

"Not me," he said. "4-F."

"Lucky guy."

He flushed again, one of the perils of being red-headed. "Not so much," he said. He turned to another patron, limping on a bum pin I hadn't noticed before.

This was shaping up to be a swell night.

Thinking it was no coincidence that Inez Ravenswood had asked me to this particular place, and knowing young Hammie's rumored predilection for drink, I did some basic detective calculations and concluded that my subject might be a known associate of the Blue Angel crowd.

I signaled Red over again, waving a tenner as incentive. He came.

"One more," I said. "Keep the change."

Forget music. Nothing soothes the savage breast like cash money. For no extra charge, Red poured me a double with a smile. But the smile turned to puzzlement when I showed him young Ravenswood's photo.

"You ever see this guy?"

He blinked at the photo—once, twice. "What is this, a joke?"

"Why, is he that funny-looking?"

"No," he said warily. "Not to me."

"So, is he a regular?"

"Yeah. Sure. Used to be in here all the time."

"Why 'used to be'? When did you last see him?"

"Come on, what's the gag?"

I was beginning to think I couldn't get a straight answer if I called Correct Time. What was it about this Ravenswood that threw everybody for a loop?

"Just answer the question."

"Okay. A week ago Thursday."

"How do you happen to remember the exact night?"

"Made a big scene with some dame. Ask one of the Domino brothers. They could tell you."

"Who?"

"The bouncers." He nodded behind me. Without turning around, I looked in the nearest mirror and saw two dangerous-looking blacks standing against a wall, their fedora-shaded eyes fixed squarely on my back.

44

"Tough-looking mugs."

"Keechie and T-Dub," the bartender said helpfully. "They're all right. It's One-Eye you got to watch out for."

"Thanks for the tip."

I stole another glance in the mirror to see if they were still watching me, but their hawk's eyes had trained on other prey. I followed their gaze across the ballroom and spotted Hellen Vergos, seated at a table under the sheltering fronds of a palm with a natty little man twenty years her senior. Was it another coincidence, or another piece of a puzzle that seemed to get bigger every time I looked at it? I wondered what the overwrought girl who had cried over lost love in my office only yesterday was doing out on the town with a fancy escort tonight. I also wondered why the Dominos seemed to find her as interesting as I did.

The man said something to her, leaning close, and she smiled, her hand resting lightly in his. I felt an unaccountable twinge. Seeing young girls with older men always seemed to bring out my big brother instincts.

She called to a waiter, handed him something, and nodded toward the bandstand. A special request?

"Say," I said to the bartender, "You see that couple over there?"

The bartender glanced in the direction I indicated and shrugged at a glass he was suddenly very interested in polishing.

"Look, Mac, I don't see nothing I ain't paid to see."

"The girl's a friend of mine, but I don't recognize the guy."

"I'm not wanting to get in the middle of no lovers' quarrels, okay?"

I frowned at him. He was as wearying as a hand-cranked jalopy.

Dahlia finished another song, and I joined in the applause as the bandleader announced a short break. Maybe I should have been watching Hellen Vergos, but I wanted to see Dahlia's reaction to the note. The waiter brought it over to her on a silver platter, like it was the latest creation from the chef. Dahlia took it, read it, and frowned. The "special request" seemed to be something she wasn't too keen on. Whatever it said, she made no reply, just stuffed it in her bra as she glared right at Hellen's table. So they knew each other, that much was sure.

When I looked back, Hellen Vergos and her friend were beating it out the back way, too far across the crowded ballroom for me to catch them. So I went instead for the jazz singer. She was slowed down by some admirers, and I was able to intercept her just before she made it backstage.

"Miss Dahlia! Oh, Miss Dahlia!"

She turned a cool eye on me. "Yes?"

"Gee, that was wonderful, Miss Dahlia," I gushed, pulling out a pad and pen. "May I have your autograph?"

She gave me a tolerant smile and reached for the pen and paper. I surprised her, grabbing her wrist and hustling her out of sight behind the bandstand.

"Let go of me! What do you want?"

She struggled to break free, but I held her tight.

"Keep it down, I just want to ask you some questions."

"What are you, a cop?"

She seemed to drop the thermostat a couple degrees, as if cops were a legitimate worry for her. If she wanted to think I was a cop, I let her.

"What's your connection to Hellen Vergos?"

"I don't know what you're talking about."

"Don't hand me that. I just saw you get a note from her."

"What note?"

I nodded at her cleavage. "That note. You want I should retrieve it for you?"

Her eyes narrowed. "You're no cop."

She made a spasm to break loose again, but I held on until I felt her suddenly relax. I pulled back, saw her eyes fixed on a spot about six inches above my head, a smile playing across her lips. I could feel something looming over me and turned to find all three Domino brothers—Keechie, T-Dub, and the aptly named One-Eye—glowering down at me. Each one was bigger and meaner looking than the other, each holding his fists before him, adjusting identical pairs of domino cufflinks.

"Must be the minstrel show," I quipped. My idea of an icebreaker.

They didn't smile, but they didn't pound me into butter, either, which I took as a positive sign.

"The Boss wants to see you," said the one called Keechie.

"If you don't mind, fellas, I'm waiting for a lady."

"Looks like you been stood up," said the one called T-Dub.

I was about to continue the discussion, but One-Eye grunted a command, and I was gripped by a six-handed vise.

"Easy, easy!" I protested. "No need for bloodshed."

"Don't hurt him too bad, boys," Dahlia said merrily as they carried me away.

There were murmurs from the crowd, but the Dominos ignored them as they aimed me toward a flight of stairs opposite the bandstand, me struggling to keep my toes touching the floor. I stumbled over every third step, but with the Dominos' kind assistance made it to the top, where there was another cushioned leather door, similar to those at the club entrance, but smaller and pearl white.

T-Dub pushed it open. "Boss's office," he said helpfully.

A moment later I found myself clamped into an overstuffed chair that might have been pretty comfy were it not for Keechie and T-Dub each leaning on a shoulder like they thought I was a jack-in-the-box ready to spring. One-Eye blocked the door, casually picking his fingernails with a switchblade. Herr Doktor Geiger leaned against a mahogany desk and studied my credentials through a monocle.

Aside from the goons, the office was pretty posh, a gentleman's study that looked out on a dance floor instead of a fief. The carpets were thick and Persian, the chairs plush, the curtains deep blue damask, and the burled, mahogany desk ornately carved with oak leaves, stag horns, and other gewgaws.

In fact, Geiger himself was positively decorative in white tie and tails. With his bullet head, close-cropped hair, and shaving-brush mustache, he was a Prussian nobleman from Central Casting. But when he opened his mouth his recent past betrayed him, his accented English part Nazi kommandant, part Bowery hoodlum.

"So, you're a detective, huh?" He kept eyeing my open wallet, like he expected it to answer for me.

"What of it?"

No look, no change of expression, no word. One-Eye closed his switchblade, took three long but unhurried steps toward me, and rocked my head with a backhand slap.

It took me a few seconds to shake out the cobwebs. I licked something wet and warm off my lip, forced my eyes to focus on One-Eye's face, and smiled. He smiled back. Two professionals expressing mutual appreciation. Then I professionally stomped him in the privates. He folded like a trick chair.

His brothers laughed raucously. I turned my grin on Geiger, but he simply polished his monocle, showing no interest in me or his henchmen.

Then, like a felled sequoia righting itself, One-Eye straightened to his full height.

His brothers kibitzed hilariously:

"Uh-oh!"

"Lawd have mercy!"

"Lawd better, 'cause One-Eye ain't!"

One-Eye flicked open his knife and carved a lazy circle in the air.

"You kicked mine," he said with a grim smile. "Now I'm a-cut yours off."

I squirmed, but Keechie and T-Dub held me like a pagan sacrifice, each hooking me with a leg, forcing me spread-eagle. One-Eye brought the knife down slowly, his empty socket palpitating with anticipation. His brothers grinned salaciously as the knife pressed against my fly.

Then Geiger replaced his monocle as indifferently as he had removed it and said, "All right, boys, that's enough."

One-Eye grinned at me, no trace of disappointment on his face. With a flick of his blade he relieved me of a fly button, his amused expression seeming to say, "Next time."

"Was he packing?" Geiger asked.

One-Eye said, "Yeah, Boss," and handed Geiger the .45.

"I've got a permit for that," I said.

"Not in my club you don't."

He adroitly unsheathed the clip and emptied the chamber. Opening a cabinet behind his desk, he placed the gun among an odd collection of ugly weapons and pretty women's shoes. I didn't want to think much about how he'd accumulated either.

He tossed my wallet in my lap and ordered the Dominos to stand down. One-Eye went back to his post at the door. Keechie and T-Dub released their grip but remained as my bookends.

Geiger leaned back against his desk, his pose fatherly, but his tone dangerous, like Judge Hardy with a knife up his sleeve. "I don't like detectives snooping around my joint." He said "detectives" as "detectiffs."

"So I gather."

"You're a smart guy, aren't you?"

"Smart enough to know the reason I'm here isn't just because I'm a detective."

"The reason you are here is exactly why you are here."

He made this pronouncement like it was the wisdom of the ages. I didn't get it, so I didn't say anything.

"You were meeting someone." He said "were" as "vhere."

"Yeah."

"Who?"

"I'd say none of your business—" I could feel the Dominos coil like cobras around me. "But I've only got two more buttons on these pants. I was meeting Inez Ravenswood."

The monocle gleamed. "Yes. Fortunately for you, I intervened."

"Why fortunately?"

"Let's just say that men who show undue interest in Mrs. Ravenswood have a tendency to very short life spans."

"She's that dangerous?"

"No. But I am."

He wasn't subtle, but I got the point.

"I assure you," I said with a straight face, "my interest in Mrs. Ravenswood is purely professional."

"As is hers in you, I am sure." He said "sure" as "shu-ah," like a Five Points urchin.

"She's paid you, then?" he continued. "For some...professional service?"

"Actually...no."

"That must be a very strange profession you have. One that doesn't pay."

"Yeah. You could say that."

"Get this," he said, with sudden heat. "Mrs. Ravenswood belongs—she belongs completely and utterly—to me."

"Funny, I had the quaint idea Mrs. Ravenswood belonged to Mr. Ravenswood."

I thought I might get another smack for that one, but Geiger only snorted in amusement.

"A rich man thinks he can buy anything," he philosophized. "But a woman like Inez Ravenswood can only be rented."

"So what's your trick?"

Geiger smiled oilily. "Ruthlessness, Mr. York. Only through ruthlessness can one possess such a woman. I trust I make myself clear?"

"Crystal."

"Then my friends will show you out."

"Front or back, Boss?" T-Dub asked.

Geiger feigned a kindly smile. "Since our meeting has been so amicable...Front."

They showed me out front, all right—then sent me headlong into a couple of trashcans.

I heard titters from a clutch of new arrivals, and someone cracked, "Looks like we missed all the fun."

"Say, pal," quipped another. "Did you leave any for us?"

Splayed out in the dirt, sitting square on my dignity, I couldn't do much but let them have their laugh.

One-Eye skimmed my fedora onto my lap, and with an unnerving, Cyclops wink, turned back toward the club with his brothers. I saluted their retreating backs and said, "Thanks, fellas. It's been a pleasure."

I got up, dusted myself off, and checked my watch. As delightful as I'd found the ambiance at Geiger's club, it was time to beat it to Mulholland Drive.

-8-

Traffic was light, and the Packard purred easily as it climbed the hills of Laurel Canyon. I watched the slide show of the twinkling city lights in my rearview mirror, blinking in and out with every curve. I couldn't shake the feeling that I was being followed, but aside from the occasional jackrabbit, the road was empty and still.

I'd wanted to get to the rendezvous early so I could case the layout, but when I pulled up at the crossroads of Laurel Canyon and Mulholland, a long, two-tone Cadillac was already waiting, parked in the dirt.

A natty, little man wearing a gray pinstripe suit and carrying a brown satchel got out of the Caddy and came up to my window with hand extended, like he meant to ask for my vote for City Council.

"You York?"

"Yeah."

He pumped my hand. "Fred Fergus. Mind if we take your car?"

"Hop in."

He hopped.

"Nice night for a little cloak-and-dagger, eh?"

"Not bad," I said.

Leaning forward, he peered up through the windshield at the sky. Low clouds had begun to drift in from the sea.

"Kind of dark."

"That happens, sometimes," I said. "At night."

He blinked at me.

"So, Mr. Fergus, you want to fill me in on what we might expect?"

"Fred," he said. "My friends call me Freddy. You?"

"Me what?"

"You got a name?"

"Ellis. And my friends do *not* call me Elly."

"Fair enough."

"So?"

"A simple exchange. That's it."

"Which way?"

"Straight ahead. I'll tell you where to turn."

As Fergus pointed the way down the twisting canyon roads, scrutinizing every road sign, I sized him up out of the corner of my eye. He wore his hat canted on the back of his head, so his face was easy to make out in the glow of the dashboard lights. His eyes squinted over a long rat's nose, like a marksman looking down a barrel. Under his rat's nose was a rat's whisker of a mustache that only accentuated his rat-like overbite. So I guess "rat" pretty much summed him up in the looks department. But he didn't look dangerous. I could see him as somebody's pet. I could see "Freddy."

He'd changed out of the formal wear, but the moment I laid eyes on him I pegged him for Hellen Vergos' escort from the Blue Angel. If he knew me or knew that I knew him, he'd given no indication. Fine with me. If he wanted to play dumb, so could I.

Despite the hale-fellow act when he came up to my car, it was obvious he was nervous. His eyes nictitated against the gloom like it was high noon in the Mojave, and he clutched the satchel against his chest with both arms wrapped around it.

He caught me eyeing him, but apparently took my look for a question.

"It's not far. Just up the canyon a little ways."

"Why such an out-of-the-way place?"

"Oh, prying eyes, all that."

I didn't like it. The best way to make an exchange like this is under bright lights, with lots of witnesses. This smelled like a double-cross.

"Not afraid, are you?"

I looked at his grip on the satchel. White knuckles.

"I've felt better," I said. "You?"

"This isn't my usual line."

"What is your usual line?"

He breathed a self-consciously breezy note. "Ohhh, torts, contracts, that sort of thing."

I played more dumb than usual. "Lawyer, huh?"

"Off-i-cer of the Court," he pronounced with a nasal chuckle, checking to see if I got the irony.

"So long as the Court and the Colonel see eye-to-eye, huh?"

"Oh, that's *never* a problem," he said. Then with another chuckle, he added, "Not for the Colonel, anyway."

I chuckled along with him. We were simpatico, just two working stiffs on the Big Man's payroll.

I nodded at the satchel. "That the money?"

"Yeah. Wanna have a look?"

"I've seen money before."

"Not a hundred thousand dollars, I bet."

I pursed my lips in a silent whistle. The Packard's tires did a drumroll as the blacktop turned to gravel.

"Stay straight," he told me.

"You know," I said, "The Colonel doesn't strike me as the kind of guy willing to pay for the same thing twice."

"The Colonel's a pragmatist," Fergus said so quickly it sounded rehearsed. "A hundred G's is nothing."

"May be," I said skeptically. "But it's a lot of nothing."

"This is it."

He indicated a sign that read, "DEAD END."

I eyed the sign grimly and turned the wheel.

"Up ahead." He pointed past a single, low-slung ranch house with dimly glowing windows to the dark end of the cul-de-sac. "You see the light post?"

"I see a post."

"They said the light would be out, to park under it."

"Great," I said. "Do you mind telling me who this 'they' is we're going to meet?"

"They're the people who have the Colonel's merchandise."

"More than one."

"Definitely.

"They got names?"

"That's confidential."

"So you know who they are?"

"I didn't say that."

"Perfect."

As we approached the end of the cul-de-sac, I saw broken glass glittering in the gravel ahead. It looked like somebody had shot out the light. I cocked the wheel to the right to avoid the glass and cut the headlights, my intention to roll up as inconspicuously as possible.

"Turn your lights back on," Fergus snapped.

"And why would I do that?"

"They want to be able to see us."

I flicked them back on. "Of course they do."

We rolled to a stop under the shot-out street lamp, the lights of the Packard blazing out into the gloom.

"Shall I crank up the radio, too?"

"Cut your engine. Then flash your lights once and leave them off."

I did as I was told.

"Now what?"

"We wait."

"For what, a signal or a rub-out?"

He looked at me, squeezed out two nasal notes. "You have a dark sense of humor."

"Yeah, well. It's a dark night."

Fergus' white-knuckled fingers fretted, crab-like, around the edges of the satchel as he squinted out into the darkness.

"The signal should come any second."

I reached across to the glove box and pulled out a flashlight, covered the lens with my hand, flicked it on and off.

"I hope you're packing more than a flashlight."

I didn't answer. The push of a button on the steering column flipped out a panel from under the dashboard, my emergency spare clipped inside. A snub-nosed Smith & Wesson, thirty-eight caliber.

"Nice," Fergus said.

The pistol came loose in my hand with a click, and I checked the cylinder. Five slugs, an empty chamber under the hammer. The gun was too small for my forty-five's shoulder holster, so I just held it in my hand, finger off the trigger, cradled against my stomach.

Fergus sat up and pointed. "There it is."

Down in the canyon, the yellow glow of a lantern swung to and fro.

Fergus turned to me, his breath coming a little fast, his fingers fretting at the satchel like it was an unruly fiddle. He didn't say anything, so I said, "Let's go."

I got out, flashlight in my left hand, gun in my right, and stepped to the edge of the road where the ground sloped sharply downward. Fergus followed my lead, still clutching the satchel to his chest, his arms crossed over it as if he were afraid someone might try to snatch it from him.

I crouched down so as not to make too clear an outline against the sky. Fergus did likewise. The signal lamp had gone dark, and we waited for it to show again.

"There," I said. I flicked on my flash and swept it once over the ground before us, just enough to get a bearing. "Looks like they're at the end of this trail."

"After you," Fergus said.

I led the way, but we didn't make it three yards before we were stumbling and sliding over the scrub oak and loose earth. "We'll have to use the light," I growled, "before we break our necks. Try to stay low."

"Sure," he said. "Whatever you say."

The flash made a dazzling pool in the inky blackness. I pointed it almost straight down, giving us just enough light to see our feet, trying to keep it at the edge of my peripheral vision so I wouldn't go completely night blind.

Up ahead, the beacon would flicker a moment, then go out, then after a few seconds flicker again. That kept us going in the right direction without allowing us to pin down exactly where it was. I thought of all the little presidents snuggled so warm and cozy in the safe at my office, and wished I was there with them.

A sudden noise to the left of the trail. I dropped to one knee, swinging flashlight and pistol around in one motion. Fergus dropped to the ground beside me, curled around the satchel like a frightened possum.

Reflecting back the beam of the flash were two glowing animal eyes. The creature froze in mid-step, its outline indistinct in the brush, eerie eyes fixed. It snorted two puffs of breath that shimmered in the beam of the flash, then skittered away into the dark.

"Just a coyote," I said.

"Is it dangerous?"

"I'm guessing not as dangerous as what's up ahead."

A whistle came to our ears, and the lantern swung in a long, emphatic arc.

"Destiny calls," I said.

Fergus smiled wanly, and I helped him to his feet.

We trudged forward about forty more yards, but the beacon had gone dark again. No more helpful flickers or whistles to guide us. When we came to a flat, sandy spot where the scrub oak had been cleared away, I stopped and killed the flash. Again I crouched down, and Fergus crouched beside me, practically in my back pocket.

"I thought it was just about here," I said.

"I can't see a thing," Fergus complained. "Turn your light back on."

"We're already sitting ducks out here. No need to make it too easy for them."

We waited. Not a sound, not a flicker of light anywhere. But I could feel eyes on me, waiting for nothing in particular, just making us sweat.

A blazing white spotlight hit us like a punch in the face, and I instinctively went to one knee and swung my gun toward it.

"I wouldn't, gumshoe."

I froze, my eyes tearing up in the glare. Behind the light, not even a shadow was visible.

"Drop the gat on the ground," the voice said. "Nice and easy."

I dropped.

"The flash, too."

I did.

"Good boy. Now stand up. Keep your hands where I can see them."

I stood, I kept.

"Now you, shyster. Toss me the bag."

Fergus hadn't moved since the light hit us, and he made no sign of moving now. I couldn't see a thing, but I had a sense the voice was alone. There was an air of the bluff about it, a little too gruff, too commanding. Figuring his attention was on Fergus, I lowered my right hand, just a couple inches, trying to shade my eyes from the glare. But no dice.

"Keep 'em up, gumshoe," the voice barked. "And you, shyster. For the last time. Toss me the bag."

Fergus still didn't move, still held the bag against his chest. If I hadn't been so focused on the man behind the light, I might have noticed Fergus now had only one arm wrapped around the satchel.

"Do you have the package?" I could see Fergus shaking, and his voice had a distinct tremolo.

"Yeah, I got it. You don't think I'd double-cross you, do you, shyster?"

"Let's see it."

I looked at Freddy's rodentate profile. He had more brass than I'd figured.

A long pause from the voice behind the light. Then a flat rectangle floated out of the darkness and plopped into of the pool of light, kicking up a swirl of dust. Freddy eyed it, just five paces away.

"Your turn," the voice said.

But Freddy still didn't move, still held the satchel tight. I could feel the voice's gun, as sure as if it were pressed against my belly, and I didn't like the way the little lawyer was stretching this out.

"Where's the girl?" he said.

I looked at him. The first girl I thought of was Hellen Vergos, but he'd just been with her, so that didn't figure. I wanted to tell the voice I needed to confer with my client, but I didn't think he'd go for it.

"What do you care?" the voice said.

"The agreement was that I would deal only with the girl."

"First I heard of it."

I knew just how he felt.

"That was the agreement."

"Well, we'll just have to agree to disagree, then, won't we? Now gimme."

"Better do as he says," I said out of the corner of my mouth.

Fergus ignored me. "I know it's you, Guy."

Something tingly crawled up my spine and under my hat. My eyes flicked involuntarily between Fergus, the light, and my gun, as my nerves sounded red alert.

"I'm counting to three, shyster."

"I recognize your voice, Guy."

I looked hard at Fergus, but he was oblivious, his eyes as fixed on the light as the coyote's had been.

"One."

I gauged the angles. The spotlight was maybe twenty feet away, my gun six or eight.

"The Colonel's going to be very disappointed, Guy."

"Two."

I braced myself, determined not to wait on "three," but Fergus was ahead of me. His free hand—the one I hadn't noticed had let go of the satchel—produced a pistol and fired.

I dove for my gun as the light went out, my aim to grab it and roll, ready to shoot, but I never got the chance. Guns exploded—I don't know how many—the muzzle flashes whirling around me like Mexican fireworks. I got off a couple of shots, but mostly I just tried to stay out of the way until the shooting stopped.

When it did, I kept still, hugging the dirt. I heard running footsteps, car doors and engines. I heard moans.

Scrabbling through the dirt, I found my flashlight, flicked it on.

The moans were coming from Freddy Fergus. He lay sprawled on his back, his eyes wide, blinking up at the sky. Blood flecked his lips, oozed through his fingers where one hand clutched his chest.

"Hang on, pal," I said. "I'm gonna get some help."

I flicked my light out in little arcs on the ground around us, caught the soles of two shoes.

This one had a hole in his neck. Drained of blood, his face shone in the light like a porcelain bowl in a black pool. I didn't recognize him, but the broken spot and the rectangular package told me it was the voice behind the light. I checked his I.D. Licensed to carry. Name of Guy Pollone.

I squatted over the package. It was a leather pouch, the letters HHR in gold monogram above the curled figure of a ram's horn.

But when I opened it I found no jeweled sculpture. Instead there were photographs, maybe a couple dozen. Flipping through them, I saw two figures in various states of nakedness, clenched in the throes of love-making. The photos all seemed to depict the same place—some overstuffed boudoir—but the lighting and bits of clothing differed from shot to shot, indicating they had been taken on different occasions. The girl looked to be no more than sixteen, her eyes closed in every pic, her dark skin almost white in the glare of the flash. I mightn't have recognized her at all had it not been for the flower in her hair.

The man I didn't know, but he looked familiar. He was white but well tanned, with long, sinewy limbs and the dashing profile of an aging stage actor. I started flipping back through the photos, looking for one with a good angle on his face, when I heard a step behind me.

I whirled in time to see something big and black swing down on me with something heavy and hard.

-9-

I woke up to distant alarms sounding in my throbbing head. Something wet behind my ear. Dirt in my mouth. I tried to push myself up, but the arm underneath me was lifeless and tingling, a heavy weight pressed in its hand. I struggled to raise it and found I was still holding my thirty-eight.

I looked at it dumbly, then past it, my eye caught by the oblique beam of the flash where it lay on the ground. Following the beam, I looked straight into the dead eyes of Freddy Fergus. But he hadn't bled to death. There was another hole to match the one in his chest, this one square in the middle of his forehead.

I didn't need Perry Mason to tell me the bullet in Freddy's brain had come from my own trusty thirty-eight. I struggled to my feet, picked up the flash, and swept it unsteadily over the area. Pollone was still there, no extra bullet holes in him. But the money was gone, the package gone. The alarm in my head started to sound like police sirens, and I knew I had better be gone, too.

One last look at Freddy Fergus. His eyes stared toward heaven with the disappointment of the dead.

"Sorry, Freddy," I said. "Tough break."

I made my way back up the trail as quickly as I could, my breath labored, my head pounding. The sirens were getting louder, and I expected the cops any minute. What I didn't expect, when I got back to the road, was to find the Packard gone.

My aching brain whirled. I couldn't figure the angles on this one, and for the moment, I didn't even try. No time to panic, no time even to curse my luck.

I hustled up the road, just making it to the front gate of the ranch house at the corner, when a flotilla of squad cars came roaring down the canyon. Ducking behind some trashcans, I let the cops roll by. When they were out of sight, I broke down the thirty-eight, dropped a piece in each can. Farther up the road were two more houses, two more sets of trash cans. I disposed of the rest of the pieces of the incriminating weapon and made my getaway.

Somehow, I managed to make it all the way back down to Franklin without being seen or passing out. I spotted a phone booth in the parking lot of an all-night restaurant called The Gingerbread House. The lot was full, even at this time of night, the place lit up like a fairy tale and bursting with music and laughter.

I stumbled into the phone booth and fished a nickel out of my pocket. There were people I usually called when I found myself in a fix like this, but I decided instead to call the person who had gotten me in it in the first place. The phone rang seven times before the line was picked up and a languid female voice said, "Hullo."

"This is York. We need to talk."

Pause. "Now? What time is it?"

"I'm at The Gingerbread House, on Franklin. You know it?"

"Yes, but—"

The booth pitched under me like a dinghy in a squall. I dropped the phone, bracing myself against the glass as Hellen Vergos' voice called to me. Breathing heavily, my knees wobbling, I looked at the swinging receiver, at the inviting warmth of The Gingerbread House. If I reached down for the phone, maybe I wouldn't make it back up. If I staggered toward the restaurant, maybe I wouldn't make it to the door. I don't remember choosing, but when I came back to my senses, the booth I found myself in featured not a phone, but leatherette seats and a steaming cup of coffee.

The Gingerbread House was one of those Hollywood "theme" restaurants built by the frustrated set designers that pass for architects out here. The fancifully carved wood of the beams and furnishings was about as real as the sugar frosting that decorated the gingerbread roof. But the candy-tinted windows had a warm glow, and the sign out front promised "World Famous Pastries and Pies," so you just knew the service was friendly and the food was good.

Even at this late hour the place was lively, the patrons as rosy with liquor and good cheer as the apple-cheeked children, smiling hags, and dancing bears that cavorted through the wraparound murals. A strolling accordion player tickled out requests as he made the rounds among the tables and booths. Aside from the inevitable tourists, the patrons were a mixture of North European ex-pats and lonely-clubbers from flat, cold places like Wisconsin and North Dakota, who got together every week for Schlitz and schnitzel, or maybe Schnapps and strudel, and endless requests of "Liebestraum."

The front doorbell tinkled, and I saw Hellen Vergos scanning the faces that greeted her, standing on tiptoe to see to the back. I leaned forward out of the shadow and waved her over.

She came toward me, moving like a dark angel through the crowd of flushed, red faces. Her coat was simple, and her plain hat cut an attractive angle over eyes that needed no liner or mascara to stand out across the room. Nor was there a hint of gloss on her lips, nor rouge on her cheeks, and yet she had the eye of every man in the place.

"Are you all right?" she said, sitting across from me.

"I'm fine. Keep your voice down." I sat back in the shadow and pulled my hat lower over my face.

She glanced over her shoulder, then back at me. "Is something wrong?"

I suppressed a sharp remark and settled for mild sarcasm. "You could say that."

"What happened?"

"Not much. I just woke up from a nap with a couple of stiffs."

"Stiffs? You mean, dead people?"

"They don't come any deader."

I tapped out a smoke, offered her one, but she demurred. I lit up, took a drag, gave her plenty of time, but she didn't seem inclined to hold up her end of the conversation.

"Your next question should be something on the order of who, what, when, where, and why."

She looked defensive, maybe a little frightened. "But what does it have to do with me?"

62

"A 'what' question. That's good, but maybe I should be asking you."

"Stop toying with me!"

"I said keep your voice down."

She stared at me, real anger in her eyes.

"Okay, fair enough," I said. "One of the stiffs was a fellow by the name of Guy Pollone."

She couldn't hide her surprise, but tried to play it cool.

"Guy Pollone?"

"Yeah, you know him?"

"Not personally. He used to work for Col. Ravenswood. They had a falling out."

"I figured. The Colonel make a habit of that?"

"Of what?"

"Falling out with people."

Her lips crooked into a half-smile. "You could say that."

"Maybe you know the other one. He used to work for the Colonel, too. A lawyer. Name of Fergus."

Her hand went to her mouth. "Oh, my!"

She stared at me. I stared back.

"No, it can't be."

I kept staring.

"Freddy's...dead?"

She put her face in her hands. I hate to be cynical—okay, I love to be cynical—but it was all by the book, every move. But if it was a show, it was a good one. The tears were real.

A waitress came up, pot in one hand, cup and saucer in the other, a friendly greeting on her lips. But she balked when she saw Hellen sobbing. Instead of speaking or going on her way, she just stood gaping, her eyes bouncing from Hellen, to me, and back.

People were starting to look our way, so I barked, "Can't you see the lady needs a cup of coffee?"

The waitress "yessired" me, put down the cup, and poured. Hellen managed a "Thank you" between sniffles.

She let the cup warm her hands for a moment, then ventured a sip, frowned, added some cream, all without looking me in the eye.

"I saw you tonight at the Blue Angel." I had her attention, but still no eye contact. "Why'd you duck me?"

Looking up now, her eyes all innocence. "I didn't know you were there."

"Uh-huh. I also saw you slip a note to the jazz singer. She a friend of yours?"

A pause. "You could say we go back a ways."

Something there, a sardonic edge to her voice, like a smudge on a milk glass.

"And what about Fergus? How far back do you go with him?"

She lifted her cup, grimaced, put it down. "I need a drink."

I let my face show my genuine surprise. "That's funny. I never figured you for the gin and jazz type. You seem more like church and chocolate milk."

I didn't really mean anything by it, but my words seemed to cut. She covered up with a crooked smile.

"Even when you don't know what you're saying, you're cruel."

Now I was the one who felt cut. "I don't mean to be."

Her smile softened, and she laid a hand on mine.

"I believe that," she said. "You're not so different from Freddy, really. He had his rough edges, but he was kind to me at a time I most needed it."

She kept her hand on mine, and I let it stay. I liked it. It was a perfect little thing, and it gave me a warm feeling.

The accordion player sidled up to our table, dithering a schmaltzy tune, the smile under his waxed mustache kind and knowing. In the warm, butterscotch light, Hellen's face was a soothing dream after a troubled night's sleep. But when I looked at her, maybe a little too deeply, her eyes fell and she pulled her hand away.

I fished a coin out of my pocket and dropped it in the can on the accordion player's belt. With a flourish of reedy notes and a bow of his head, he took his leave.

My companion suddenly seemed very interested in straightening the pleats of her skirt. I sat back, took a lazy drag on my cigarette, enjoying the schoolgirl act, if act it was. Aware of my eyes on her, she let the skirt go, dabbed with her napkin at a drop of coffee on her saucer. Then a showy, sheepish look.

"This place is kind of corny, isn't it?"

I kept my eyes on her in a way my mother once told me was rude. "I don't know," I said, offering a little shrug. "I kind of like it. It's the sort of place you can forget your troubles, pretend the whole world is malted milk and Mom's apple pie."

I meant it. The people and their good cheer seemed real enough, even if everything else was plaster and papier-mâché. But Hellen Vergos took no notice, her eyes squarely on mine now.

"I can never seem to tell whether you're serious or joking."

I took in another lungful of nicotine, breathed it out my nose.

"One thing you can count on with me," I said. "I'm always—"

Funny, I don't know whether I intended to say "I'm always serious" or "I'm always joking." Hellen Vergos interrupted the thought with a gasp.

"You're bleeding!"

Following her eyes, I touched a soft, wet spot behind my ear, came away with red-tipped fingers.

Hellen pulled a handkerchief from her pocketbook, handed it to me with a wry smile.

"Here," she said. "Towel yourself down."

I took it from her, pressed it against the wound, made a face that was probably half-wince, half-smile. "Thanks."

She leaned over the table to have a better look, frowned at what she saw.

"You need medical attention."

She fished a bill from her pocketbook, dropped it on the table.

"Come on."

-10-

Hellen Vergos' little Olds coupè rocked as gently as a cradle, and the drive to her apartment was short and pleasant as an afternoon nap. The night clerk was on duty at the Denmark Arms, and considering the late hour, I wasn't surprised when my hostess hurried me past his desk like a sorority girl sneaking a boyfriend past the house matron.

Once we were safely in the stairwell she said, "I don't think he saw us."

"What if he did? Is he your boyfriend?"

"No," she said, adding pointedly, "And neither are you."

"So?"

"So, they're kind of protective of me around here. You know—a single girl, no family."

"Like Little Orphan Annie."

"Yeah," she said at the top of the stairs. "Like Little Orphan Annie."

She showed me into her apartment, a large, bachelor-style arrangement with a kitchenette and a parlor area that doubled as sleeping quarters when the Murphy bed was down. There was no dresser or chifforobe, so I figured the extra door in the back wall must have been a dressing room. The sofa and other furnishings were modest but new and tastefully matched. It wasn't exactly the Ritz, but it wasn't the YWCA either.

She pulled a chair out from the dinette and ordered me to strip off my shirt and sit. A minute later she had a bowl of water and a bottle of alcohol and was gently patting the swollen egg behind my ear with a damp towel.

"How am I, Doc?"

"You'll live." She pulled back, inspecting her work. "I don't have a bandage to cover that cut, but I think it'll be all right. At least the bleeding's stopped."

She exchanged the towel for a cotton ball, which she doused with alcohol. The smell of it tickled my nose as she brought it up, but the sting as it touched my head was no tickle. I yelped.

"Don't be a baby."

"Yes, ma'am."

She dabbed at the wound a few more times, as if to test me, then folded the pinkish ball in a tissue. "There," she said.

"Thanks."

She took the balled-up shirt from my lap and held it up to assess the damage. "I'll wash the blood out of this collar. It'll only take a minute. Make yourself at home."

As she went to the sink and ran some water I got up and tapped out a cigarette. "Mind if I smoke?"

"Not at all." She saw me patting my pockets for a match. "There're matches on the credenza."

I wasn't sure what a credenza was, but I saw the matches. I lit up, dropped the match in an ashtray. Next to the ashtray was a crystal atomizer. I picked it up and gave it a sniff. The smell—musky, tropical, with a hint of orchid—yanked me back across the years, images floating before me of late nights and confused emotions, of a woman who drank too much and cared too little. It was the same stuff my mother used to wear. Very expensive.

I dropped the atomizer back on the credenza with such a rap that Hellen looked up from her laundering. I forced a sheepish smile to cover.

"Sorry. What line of work did you say you were in?"

"I didn't."

"Suppose you enlighten me."

"Former secretary."

I picked up a photograph of an old, immigrant couple, their features as frankly Greek as a bottle of ouzo, posed proudly with the beautiful dark-haired little girl they had been blessed with so late in life. The frame was genuine gold leaf.

"And what are they paying former secretaries these days?"

Hellen appeared before me, shirt in hand. She took the photograph, put it back in its place.

"Your folks were good people," I said. "Hard-working."

"Yes, they were. And yes, they left me a little inheritance. And no, there's nothing left of it."

"So, what pays for this place?"

"That's a rude question."

"Ravenswood?"

Bingo.

"As a matter of fact," she said stiffly, "when I was under the Colonel's employ I was paid very well."

So that's what they called it. Under the employ.

"So, why'd you quit?"

"I didn't. When the Colonel found out Hammie was in love with me, he fired me. He said I was a gold-digger."

"But he kept paying you."

The barest flush of red brightened under her olive skin. "No, he—all right, yes, he kept paying me."

"Why?"

She faced me squarely, that old schoolmarm tone back in her voice. "You seem to forget, Mr. York, that you work for me. I don't have to answer your questions."

"Uh-huh."

"Here's your shirt."

She shoved it at me. The blood was gone, but it looked like a limp dishrag.

"No fluff-and-fold?"

The look she gave me was three seconds of very rough road, but exasperation won out over anger, and before I could laugh off the joke, she had turned back to the kitchenette. A neat little ironing rig came down out of the wall. She plugged the electric cord into the socket and smoothed the shirt out on the board as she waited for the iron to heat. Her back was turned to me, and feeling like the first-class heel that I was, I watched as she tested the iron, ran it carefully over the cloth, taking extra time on the wet collar. She was the daughter of a maid, and she knew what she was doing, but that was not her life, and I felt a strange determination—whether my own or the vibration from her soul-deep conviction—that it never would be.

I stepped up behind her and touched her arm. She spun around, startled. The look I gave her set her back a step, but the ironing board gave her nowhere to go. I crooked an arm around her and pulled her close.

"Don't."

But I did. She turned her face away, denying my kiss, and I must have balked, too, when I caught the scent of that old, familiar perfume in her hair. I could smell it even as I held my breath. I pressed her more tightly to me, finding her lips, mashing them against mine, trying to blot out the scent with the pressure of flesh on flesh. Then I felt her fists in my chest, pushing me away. The perfume was making my head spin, and I let her go.

"What are you afraid of?" I said, in a triumph of ego over matter.

She said nothing, but her eyes stayed locked with mine, her breath quick and shallow.

"Well..." I reached for her, but she turned away.

"Oh, look what you've done!"

She snatched up the iron, showing the dark brown imprint underneath. I peered at it over her shoulder, taking in the toasty aroma of scorched cotton. It was a smell I'd always sort of liked, and anyway, it killed the scent of her perfume.

She clicked off the iron, set it in the cradle, and lifted up the shirt for inspection.

"It's just on the tail. Maybe it won't show."

"It's okay," I said. "I've got six more just like it."

She smiled at that, handed it to me. I tossed it aside and took her by the wrist—but I wasn't rough about it, and she didn't pull away.

"You liked it. You know you did."

"You don't know what you're saying."

"Come on," I said, smoothing my hair. "I wasn't hit that hard."

She didn't return my smile—one of those times, I guess, when she couldn't tell whether I was joking. Her arm gave a tug, but not enough to break my grip.

"I'm still in love with Hammie."

"Now, who was talking about love?"

I probably should have gotten slapped for that one, but she just looked sad and amused. "You're really horrible sometimes, you know that?"

I bowed over her hand and kissed the back of it. "M'lady."

There was that perfume again. I straightened up too quickly, and everything went dark and wobbly.

"Are you all right?"

I pressed one hand against my temple, but the perfume was on my fingers, getting up my nose. I pulled my hand away with a jerk.

"Where'd you get that perfume you're wearing?"

The way I was behaving, I don't think she knew whether to be defensive or just bewildered.

"It was a gift. From Colonel Ravenswood."

"You should try another brand."

She looked at me a moment, picked up the phone. "I'll call you a cab."

I watched her dial the number as the room went in and out of focus.

"Yes," she said, when someone picked up. "I need a cab. The Denmark on Larchmont. Apartment 3-G."

I forced a weak smile as she hung up. "'Here's your hat, York. What's your hurry?'"

"Put on your shirt."

I struggled to put each arm through a sleeve, wobbled up against the sofa. The buttons, I decided, could wait for later.

"Can we open a window?"

She stamped across the room and threw open the sash. I stumbled over, leaned over the ledge, and breathed in the cool air.

"I'm sorry you find my scent so offensive."

After several deep breaths I felt my head clearing. "It's not that. Just my head."

She crossed her arms over her middle, debating whether to feel sorry for me or boot me out the window.

"Forget what I said, okay? I like it. The perfume. It just reminds me of someone I used to know."

"Someone horrible, I hope."

I smiled at that. "Look," I said, as gently as I could. "We should talk about some things."

"You should find Hammie. That's what I paid you for."

"That's right," I said, feeling my strength gathering with every breath. "And then I almost got myself killed. Two other guys weren't so lucky. I'm thinking there's a connection."

"Don't be ridiculous."

After a couple questions it seemed pretty clear she was in the dark about what Freddy had been up to, so I brought her up to speed. I told her about the job the Colonel hired me for, the exchange with Freddy, and how everything went haywire. As I described Freddy's death, she sat heavily on the sofa, her face pale.

"How awful."

"Yeah. But before the lights went out, I got a look at the dingus the Colonel was buying. Only it wasn't the dingus. It was photos."

"Photos?"

"Not very artistic, but vivid. Portraits of a certain jazz singer in passionate embrace with a man I didn't recognize at first."

"Colonel Ravenswood."

"That's right, only twenty years younger and minus the wheelchair."

"Well, I certainly had nothing to do with that."

I couldn't argue with her. I nodded at the decanter and glasses I'd noticed in the kitchenette. "Are those for real, or just for show?"

"What? Oh."

"Why don't you pour me one, Angel. All this talking makes me dry."

The schoolmarm in her couldn't hide her disapproval, but she got up and fetched the bottle like a good, little hostess. She presented it on a silver tray with a single glass, sitting down with it at the coffee table as if she were serving up a formal tea. I thought again how domestic she was, how good she'd be at looking after a man.

"The way I figure it," I said, settling next to her on the sofa, "the Colonel's dingus is stolen, just like he says. The thieves fence it, probably to some high-dollar collector in Europe, maybe South America. End of story."

She tipped the decanter up, poured a thimbleful. I helped her add another three fingers.

"Thanks."

I sampled the liquor, expecting maybe peach brandy, but it was genuine Kentucky bourbon. Maker's Mark, if I didn't miss my guess. I grunted my compliments.

"But that isn't the end of the story," she said, prompting.

"No. The Colonel never gives up on it. Keeps pining after it, sending out inquiries, despite his advisers telling him it's gone for good. Then along comes our blackmailer."

"Why now, after all these years?"

I shrugged. "A new bride enters the picture. Suddenly, a chanteuse in the woodpile goes from a bachelor's indiscretion to a happily married millionaire's catastrophe."

"Go on."

Maybe it was the liquor, maybe it was the thrill of a breaking case, but I felt myself warming up to my story. "Naturally, the Colonel being the kind of man he is, one doesn't just ring him up out of the phone book. There's channels. There's channels to get to the channels. And naturally, your friend Freddy, being the Colonel's lawyer, is channel number one. The next best thing to a direct line. So, the blackmailer gives Freddy his demands. Freddy relays those demands to the Colonel. Only somehow, instead of incriminating photos, the Colonel gets the idea he's buying the long lost dingus."

"You're saying Freddy double-crossed him?"

"Him and everybody else. The way I figure it, Freddy's plan was to make the trade, pop the girl, pocket the hundred G's, and hold onto the photos for future use. Only things don't go according to plan. The girl doesn't show, Freddy blows his cool, and all the wrong people wind up dead."

"I don't believe it. What could motivate him to do such a thing?"

I shrugged. "Gambling debts. Bad investments. Income tax troubles. Maybe some kind of score to settle with the Colonel. Or maybe just plain, old greed. I'm betting the motivation won't be hard to find once someone takes a look."

"But still...murder...It doesn't make sense."

"Maybe it would make sense if you told me how you were involved."

"I was only trying to protect him."

"Who, Freddy?"

"Colonel Ravenswood."

"That old war horse? Why would you want to protect him?"

"Because he—he's my father."

I whistled my surprise.

"Apparently, in his younger days, he was a man of many indiscretions."

"Well, whaddya know."

"I only learned recently. You may remember my mother—Mrs. Vergos—worked as the Colonel's maid for many years. When I was born...Well, my father—that is, Mr. Vergos—"

She was too nice to say it, so I filled in the blanks. "Yeah, Old Man Vergos wouldn't have been the type to ask questions."

She doubled over, her face pressed to her hands, but the waterworks didn't come this time. She straightened up, took a breath. "So naturally, when Hammie fell in love with me—"

"Sure," I said. "I can see why the Colonel might frown on that."

"But I had no idea. You must believe me."

"So how did Hammie take the news?"

"He was devastated. He'd asked me several times to elope with him, but...I wanted a wedding..."

You would, I thought, and felt an instant pang at my own cynicism. I couldn't help but feel sorry for the kid. "Your mother would have liked that," I said in an attempt to be kind. The words felt funny in my mouth, and she must have sensed that, because she didn't respond.

"The Colonel—his father—our father—was so cruel about it all."

I let these new facts mull a moment in another mouthful of bourbon.

"Let's get back to the blackmail. Why did Freddy bring you in on it?"

A moment's hesitation. Something there.

"I've known Dahlia for some time. Through Hammie. She was a favorite of his at the club."

"Something in common with the old man, after all, eh?"

"There's no need to be vulgar."

"Sure, sure. But I still don't get it. Why involve you?"

She suddenly spotted a ring on the coffee table. She wiped at the ring with a napkin, slid open a tiny drawer to find a coaster.

"Leave that," I said. "Why involve you?"

She thrust the drawer shut. "It's simple enough. As a woman, Freddy thought she might listen to me. And, as the Colonel's daughter...he thought I could play on her...sympathies."

I shook my head. "This guy had more angles than a Picasso. So Freddy knew about you, too."

"Of course." There was a note of defensiveness in her voice, as if she wanted to take up for the rat. "He knew all of the Colonel's business."

"Are you in the will?"

She looked at me as if I'd unbuttoned my fly.

"Come on, don't tell me a guy like Freddy had any scruples about that."

"And what about my scruples?"

I had to admire her. Her indignance seemed genuine.

"Just answer the question."

"I saw the will." The crooked smile was back. "The part about me reads like a restraining order."

I felt for her. "Yeah, it would, wouldn't it?"

"Is that all you want to know?"

"Back to the Blue Angel. So you did talk to Dahlia?"

"Yes, but she said it was too late. Someone else was involved."

"Guy Pollone."

"She wouldn't say. We assumed it was Geiger."

"Don't rule that out."

I poured another three fingers in my glass, noticing that she had slipped a coaster under it when I wasn't watching. I raised the glass, took a slug, put it back on the bare table, watched her slip the coaster back in place.

"A minute ago, when I mentioned photos, you acted surprised."

"Did I?"

"You did. But you must have known about them."

74

"Of course. That is, I had an idea. Freddy never told me exactly what it was, just that it was incriminating."

"I see."

"You sound as if you don't believe me."

"There's more to it," I said. "Something you're not telling me."

"Like what?"

"How should I know?"

"It seems to me I've told you more than enough."

"It's never enough 'til I get it all. What else?"

Instead of answering, she picked up my glass, took a hefty swig, and choked on it. I couldn't repress a laugh, but I tried to keep the edge off. "You really are church and chocolate milk."

"I detest liquor," she said bitterly. "I only keep it around for Hammie."

"You'd do a lot for Hammie."

"Anything."

Something told me that was the simple answer I was looking for. All I needed now were the details.

"Look," I said. "A minute ago...that was out of line."

"Yes, it was."

"And I want you to understand that this is strictly a professional opinion, but..."

"Just say it."

"You and Hammie...you realize that's over...Anyway, they've got laws against that sort of thing."

"I don't need the law to tell me that. But the heart's slow to catch on."

She got up from the sofa and stood looking out the window, hugging herself against the cold night air. I went to her, put my hand on the sash.

"You're cold," I said.

She nodded. I tugged at the sash, but it stuck. She lent a hand, and when the window suddenly slammed down, the momentum took her into my arms. On the pretext of keeping her from falling, I held her, looked into her eyes, but I didn't press it. As she righted herself the dark hair brushed under my nose. The perfume didn't bother me now. I could swim in it.

Then I heard a new sound—the music in my ears of her laugh.

"Your shirt," she said, giggling.

"Huh?"

"You've put it on over your suspenders."

So I had. I got a chuckle from that, too. She helped me pull it back off. Then the suspenders. But we didn't get any further. Her hand was flat against my chest, measuring my heartbeat, her eyes half-hidden under dusky lids, as if fearing to look into mine. I didn't move, just stared down at her, willing those lips to come up, on their own, to mine. Ever so slightly, her head tilted back, and I didn't hesitate. I bent to kiss her, but the sudden ring of the telephone checked me.

"Don't answer it!" I barked.

The spell was broken. She gave me a dismissive look. "Don't be silly." She picked up, listened. "It's for you."

Panic gripped me. No one knew I was here.

"Your taxi," she explained.

"Oh. Right. Tell him I'll be right down."

She did, but when I pulled on my jacket and went to the door, she said, "I wish you wouldn't go. Not just yet."

I thought of those lowered, uncertain eyes just a moment before and what they betrayed of future regret. "I think I'd better."

"But we haven't even discussed what we're going to do."

"I know. Later."

"But—"

"The meter's running."

She didn't like that. "The taxi's—or yours?"

I kissed her—brotherly so—on the cheek.

"What was that Shakespeare said about parting?"

"Call me," she said.

I chucked her under the chin, shook my head. "No, that wasn't it."

The wide-bodied Checker cab rolled up Santa Monica toward Sycamore, me lounging in the expansive back seat, feeling as cozy as a weevil in cotton. Things were looking pretty good, I thought. True, I'd muffed the exchange, the Colonel's trusted lawyer and former bodyguard were dead, and the cops were probably after me, but on the plus side I'd worked out a major piece of the puzzle. The Colonel might not like where he was in the game, but at least now he would know what the game was. Then there was Hellen Vergos. In the movies the hero always gets the girl, so if I got the girl—and it looked to me, if I didn't rush things, like I might—then in my book that made me the hero.

We passed a movie theater showing a double bill: *They Live by Night* and *Dark Passage*. Cheery stuff. But I happened to remember there was an all-night spot next door where I could get a bottle to replenish my stock, so I told the driver to pull over. A minute later I came out, a brown-bagged bottle of Jim Beam under my arm, a fresh pack of Chesterfields in my pocket, and a jaunty tune on my lips.

Then I heard a phone ring.

That cold thing gripped me again by the back of the neck. Like a character in a horror movie who just knows the monster is standing behind him but looks anyway, I turned to find a phone booth, its door already ajar, inviting me in.

I told myself it couldn't be. It was impossible. It was just one of those silly coincidences, the kind you laugh about later. But the phone kept ringing. "Ask not," they say, but you know how it is with a phone. I picked up.

"Why'd you keep me waiting?"

I had to swallow to get my voice to work. "I—I wasn't sure it was you."

I glanced around. Except for the cab, the street was deserted. "Have you got a tail on me?"

The voice laughed. "I know your every move, gumshoe."

"Are you one of Geiger's boys?" Still looking, knowing there had to be a tail.

"Yeah. We're all Geiger's boys. Especially you."

I tried to make my tone conversational. "I'm afraid I don't follow you."

"You're afraid," the voice sneered. "That's a pigeon-livered phrase."

"Ravenswood?"

"Look in your pocket."

"Col. Ravenswood, is that you?"

"Your pocket."

"Ravenswood!"

The line was dead. I hung up, caught the taxi driver eyeing me under the brim of his cap. I reached into my jacket pocket as if I expected to find a scorpion, but it was just a piece of paper.

I pulled it out. Unfolded it once, twice. Another drawing, the same rough but able hand, the same hapless little man in a fedora. This time he was caught in a spider's web. It wasn't so much the drawing that bothered me. It was the question of how it had slipped into my pocket.

When I got back in the cab I asked the driver if he had noticed anyone following us. He said no. I told him to go on to the Sycamore address, but to cut his lights and stop a few doors down. "And keep an eye out."

As soon as we turned the corner I saw it—a black sedan, parked in the shadow, two dark figures hunkered down in the front seat. I pegged them for cops. It figured. Whoever wanted to pin Freddy's shooting on me wasn't likely to rely on the cops' investigative skills to put it together. An anonymous tip was so much more efficient.

The cabbie was on the ball. "You see 'em?"

"Yeah. Keep going. Head towards Gower."

When we got to my building, I directed him to a back alley that led to the service entrance, gave him a nice tip. The door was locked, but I had a key. The night janitor was at his usual post, sound asleep, and I was careful not to wake him as I went up the steps.

Up top, the coast was clear, and I let myself into my office without turning on the lights. It was risky coming here, but if I was going to lay low for a few days, I'd want more cash than I was carrying in my pocket.

I sat behind my desk, my honest intention to go straight to the safe, but I went to the bottle instead. My old buddy Jim Beam.

I uncapped the bottle, and in the interest of saving time, decided to forgo the glass. A tip of the bottle, a swallow, a moment to let it warm me, then I'd be on my way.

Across the street they had already changed the marquee for tomorrow's feature: *Satan Met a Lady*. Next door, the "Live Girl-" sign flashed insistently.

"They should fix that sign."

I managed to jump a foot without moving an inch. Inez Ravenswood emerged from the shadow, her face wreathed in perfumed smoke. My nose must have still been full of the stuff Hellen Vergos used, because I hadn't even noticed it when I'd come in.

She glided smooth as a cat to the window, her back facing me, half obscuring the blinking neon.

"Lovely view," she said.

"That's why they get the high rent."

Above her left shoulder, the word "Live" smoldered redly in a whorl of smoke.

"Have you ever noticed," I said, "that 'live' spelled backwards is 'evil'?"

She turned to face me, a pocket-sized pistol aimed at my heart.

"What a feeble observation," she said coolly. "Like the one about God and dog."

The way I figured it, if she didn't like my conversation she could leave. I took another swig of Jim.

"Nothing to say?"

"You've got the gun, lady."

"You were with Hellen Vergos tonight."

"Is that a question?"

"It's a fact. I suppose she finally told you she was the Colonel's bastard child?"

"I don't remember it being put exactly like that. But what if she did?"

She gave me a coy smile that was more unnerving than the gun.

"She's a lovely little thing, isn't she?"

"She's all right."

"So innocent. So...pure."

"She's a peach. So what?"

"So, I'm told she's the kind of girl rich boys like to marry. But what about poor boys?"

I'm slow, but I was getting her drift.

"Tell me," she said. "When she whispered those sweet nothings in your ear, did you hear wedding bells, or a cash register's?"

"You're nuts."

"But I'm not the one in love with Hellen Vergos."

"In love with—Are you kidding?"

"You don't believe in love, I suppose."

I kept my beliefs to myself. She took a long drag on her cigarette, exhaled a blue cloud.

"Did the subject of her mother come up?"

"You can save it," I said, glad to have one on her at last. "It just happens I've known her mother since I was a kid."

"Really? Which one? The Greek maid...or the black whore?"

Click. Another piece fell into place.

I tried to hide my surprise, but she saw right through me, her look pinning me like a bug. As far as I'm concerned, the word "wicked" belongs in fairy tales, but Inez Ravenswood had a smile that could make Medusa blush.

But it wasn't just surprise at Hellen Vergos's parentage that I felt. There was something else there, something tickling at the back of my mind, something unpleasant and familiar.

"Is that disillusionment I see in your eyes, Mr. York? Has the pot of gold at the end of the rainbow suddenly lost some of its luster?"

"It doesn't mean a hill of beans to me."

"Oh, but such a big hill. And so many beans."

I answered that with another pull from the bottle. Now her look was one of disgust. I'd settle for that. Any spontaneous reaction you could get out of Inez Ravenswood, no matter how small, was a victory.

"I'd offer you one," I cracked. "But I'm fresh out of snifters."

"Ah, the famous Ellis York wit is back."

She took the bottle from me, upended it for a mighty pull, then smashed it on the floor. Through the whole maneuver, the pistol never wavered from its target. I frowned at the litter of glass and liquor. Such a waste.

"You were with Freddy Fergus when he got shot."

"I don't suppose it would do me any good to ask how you come by all this information."

"Answer the question."

"Yeah, I was with him."

"You saw the pictures."

"Yeah."

"And what else?"

"And nothing else."

"There was something in that pouch much more valuable than those photos, but now it's gone. Where is it?"

I was getting tired of this game. Besides, I didn't know what she was talking about. My eye drifted from the cold opals of her eyes to the fur-lined collar of her jacket and the jeweled ram's horn that was pinned there.

"You know, Mrs. Ravenswood, I've been meaning to compliment you on that lovely pin you're wearing. Very unusual."

She cocked her pistol, aimed it threateningly.

"One more time. Where is it?"

Usually, people who are going to shoot you don't threaten. They just shoot you. Besides, my motto is never let 'em see you sweat. So, I smiled, feeling more confident than maybe I should. But then Inez Ravenswood smiled back—in that cold, dead way of hers—and suddenly I didn't feel so sure of myself.

She pressed the barrel of the gun against my kneecap.

"The first one's just for fun."

I watched her black-gloved finger curl around the trigger, paralyzed, as if by a hypnotizing cobra. But a loud knock at the door startled us both, breaking the spell. I grabbed her wrist, twisted the gun away from her, and pulled her into my lap.

"Open up! Police!"

She didn't cry out, just hissed in my face, "You fool! If my finger had slipped—"

"Then I'd limp every time I visited you in Tehachapi."

I pocketed the gun and drew her to me, brought those cold, amused eyes just inches away from mine. I could have shot her with her own gun, just to wipe that look off her face, but instead I kissed her, because I knew that's what she wanted me to do. Her mouth was hot on mine, our bodies rubbing together like we meant to make fire. Mixing it up with Inez Ravesnwood may have been dangerous, but it wasn't complicated. There was no past, no mixed feelings, no professional ethics to clutter things up. For her it may have been a game, or it may have been practical math, but it was all animal lust for me.

The knock came louder.

"We know you're in there, York! The janitor saw you!"

We unclenched. Her eyes were ice blue under smoky lids. They made my mouth go dry, but I managed to get out a word: "So?"

"So, let them in."

I released her wrist. It glowed with four red finger marks. She slid off my knee and let me up. The knock again.

"Keep your shirt on," I called.

I shuffled over to the door and put my hand on the knob, but froze when I heard a noise behind me. I turned just in time to see the stiletto-heeled, be-furred and bejeweled millionaire's wife slip out the window onto the fire escape. My hand went instinctively to my pocket, but the gun was as gone as she was.

Some dame.

The door rattled so hard I thought the glass would break.

"Open up, or we're bustin' it down!"

"All right, all right!"

I opened the door to find two trench coats in hats. The snap-brim entered first: Lt. Guild, L.A.P.D., beady-eyed and beefy, as tall and solid as an oak door.

"Well, if it isn't my old friend, Lt. Guild!"

Guild brushed past me, the casual swipe of one gorilla-like arm nearly knocking the wind out of me.

"Whatsa matter? Ya gotta dame in here?"

Then came the bowler: Sgt. Lestrade, round faced and squinty, not quite as wide or as tall as a Buick. He sniffed the air as he butted past.

"More like he's sleeping one off."

"And his little buddy Lestrade! What a pleasant surprise!"

"Can it," Guild said. They gave the place the once-over, making faces at the stink of liquor. Lestrade found the neck of the broken bottle and held it up for Guild to see. Guild nodded knowingly and looked a question at me.

I squinted over a cocked finger, resting an imaginary pistol over one arm. "Just doing a little target practice."

Guild came over, pulled open my coat to reveal my empty holster.

"Where's your piece?"

I shrugged. "Search me."

Guild shook his head wearily, gestured at Lestrade, who patted me down.

"He's clean."

My standard response: "Mother would be so proud."

"Cut the comedy," Guild growled. "Check his desk."

Lestrade went through all the drawers, felt around under the top, and smiled the way all cops smile when they find some little something they just knew you knew they'd never find. From the holster I had fixed under the desktop he pulled out my "insurance"—an old Colt Dragoons, forty-four caliber.

"Cute," Lestrade observed, hefting the old cannon. "Who'd you get this from, General Custer?"

Actually, it had belonged to my grandfather, an old Indian fighter who'd settled these parts when Los Angeles was nothing but mesquite and Mestizos. But I figured that was my business.

"Where's the other one?" Guild barked. "You know, the one you got a permit for?"

"In my car."

They looked at each other. I didn't know what it meant.

"And where's your car?"

"Stolen."

Another look.

"When?"

"I don't know exactly."

Lestrade started scribbling in a note pad. "Go on."

"I stopped at The Gingerbread House for a cup of coffee around midnight."

"The Gingerbread House," Guild drawled. "Whaddya, playing tourist?"

"I wanted coffee. It was convenient."

"Sure, sure..."

"When I came out, the car was gone."

Without looking up from his pad, Lestrade said, "Rough neighborhood, that Hollywood Hills."

Guild gave him a look. To me, he said, "How'd you get back here?"

"A friend picked me up."

I knew the next question and cut it off. "A client. You don't get the name."

"Yeah, yeah. Did you report the theft?"

"I was about to. I wanted a drink. I dropped the bottle. That's where you two came in."

Guild said, "A very neat story."

"Except for the part about spilling the liquor," Lestrade said.

We both looked quizzically at him.

He shrugged. "Out of character."

I gave Lestrade a look of feigned hurt as Guild stared at me with hard, marble-like eyes. He summed up the esoteric ratiocinations of his mind with one well-considered word: "Yeah."

I didn't know yet what the score was. I figured they'd been tipped, but did they have anything solid? It was a cinch they hadn't found any part of my Smith & Wesson, or the cuffs would have already been on me.

"Am I being charged with something?"

I could see the dull machinery of Guild's brain turning over the possibilities of how to answer my question, but I guess it was too early in the morning for cat-and-mouse, so he settled on the straightforward approach. "We found your car parked on a dead end road off Laurel Canyon overlooking a couple of stiffs. Know anything about it?"

That one caught me right between the eyes, but in the flatfoots' book the genuine surprise I registered probably did more for my case than the neatest phony alibi. The cops finding the car was no surprise, but I'd expected it to be at the bottom of a ditch, stripped in an alley, burned in an abandoned lot, or even parked in front of police headquarters, not right back where I had left it.

"No," I said. "Why should I?"

"You in the habit of leaving your car parked at crime scenes?"

"Not lately."

Lestrade flipped his pad closed and handed me my hat.

Guild said, "Let's us take a ride."

-12-

The ride back up to Laurel Canyon was quiet, the cops tight-lipped, their radio softly playing the top forty of the early-morning Los Angeles crime scene: burglary, domestic disturbance, and one newsworthy drunk and disorderly. Something about a mid-level matinee idol in front of the Roosevelt Hotel looking for a cab and his missing pair of pants. I could imagine the chain reaction of phone calls this minor incident would set in motion: tabloid reporters, night editors, studio heads, flaks, PR people, fix-it men, maybe even a lawyer or two. But my mind was on other matters.

Someone was playing a game with me. I didn't know yet whether it was the cops, Claude Geiger, or person or persons unknown. Surely Inez Ravenswood was involved, though she obviously hadn't been the one to tip the cops. The Colonel was probably out of it, although I had trouble imagining him, as he seemed to be, in the role of gullible victim. Hellen Vergos had never been completely straight with me, but I saw her more as the storm-tossed survivor trying to keep clear of the sharks, rather than the puppet master pulling everybody's strings. Then there was the elusive Hamlet Huffington Ravenswood III. A guy that everyone knows but no one ever seems to see is a guy you'd better watch out for.

When we came to the little road to nowhere off Laurel Canyon, I took it as a good sign that the trash collectors were already there to carry away the incriminating pieces of my thirty-eight. The two cans in front of the ranch house were at that moment being upended into the truck, their contents soon to be on their way to the harbor, where they would join the thousands of tons of human waste that make Terminal Island the great monument to Western expansion that it is. As we rolled by, one of the workers raised a hand in salute and Guild and Lestrade returned the gesture in professional courtesy. My tax dollars at work.

The sun was coming up, the mist clearing, and at the end of the cul-de-sac a half-dozen official cars were visible. And right there, parked between the morgue wagon and the Chief Inspector's car, was the Packard.

"That it?" Guild asked.

"That's it," I said.

Lestrade pulled up right behind, as if he meant to block my way should I jump in and try to make an escape. The driver's side door was open, a man in a white lab coat behind the wheel, dusting for fingerprints. Otherwise, the car appeared to be exactly as I had left it: just under the shot-out streetlight, even the wheels turned to the curb.

The way it looked to me, either I was crazy, or someone had gone to a lot of trouble to make me look foolish. Or guilty. I was pretty sure I wasn't crazy, so when we got out of the squad car, the first thing I did was walk around the back of the Packard and check for any sign that it had been moved. Unfortunately, the cops had done their usual buffalo-at-the-watering-hole bit, and any telltale impressions that might have been in the gravel had been trampled.

"What're you lookin' at?" Guild asked.

"Nothing," I said.

Lestrade passed a friendly word with the lab coat, then turned to me.

"You got your keys?"

I patted my pants pocket. "Right here."

"Must of hot-wired it," Guild said.

The lab coat shook his head. "Don't think so."

Guild turned his two black marbles on me. "Anything you're not telling us?"

"Hey, it's as much a mystery to me as it is to you."

"I'll bet." He turned back to the lab coat. "Anything else, Pete?"

"Nope. It's clean."

"Whaddya mean? No prints?"

"No nothin'."

"So it's been *wiped* clean."

"That's how it looks."

All eyes were on me.

"Well, that lets me off the hook," I said.

"How do you figure?" Guild wanted to know.

I threw up my hands. "Come on…"

But, as usual, it appeared the obvious was only obvious to the pure of heart. Guild's black beads bored into me as Lestrade not-so-subtly inched around my flank. Pete eyed me like I was some interesting new specimen he wanted to get under his microscope.

"Why would I wipe my own prints off my own car?" I pleaded. "Who am I fooling?"

For a moment Guild looked stumped, but I heard Lestrade in my left ear: "Maybe it wasn't prints."

"Yeah," Guild agreed, brilliantly. "Maybe it wasn't prints. Maybe it was something else. Like blood."

"Say," Lestrade said. "What's that behind your ear?"

The two hulks converged on me, their mitts twisting my head about like a radio dial.

"Well, well, well…"

"That's some egg you got there."

"First-rate sap work, if you ask me."

"Nah, it's a pistol-butt. Look how the skin's cut."

"Lay off!" I shouted, shaking their hands off. They stepped back, looking amused and threatening at the same time.

"You think maybe you wanta change your story?" Lestrade suggested.

"Where were you before you stopped at The Gingerbread House?" Guild barked, taking the hard line.

"Come on, York, spill it."

I didn't see any reason not to. "I was at the Club Blue Angel."

"Ohhh, your *usual* hangout," Guild said, cutting a look at Lestrade.

"Pretty swanky for a low-rent dick," his partner observed.

"I was meeting a client. She didn't show."

"So?"

"So, maybe I had a few drinks. So, maybe I asked the wrong people the wrong questions."

"So, maybe you got tossed out on your ear, is that it?"

"No maybe. You can ask. There were plenty of witnesses."

"We'll do that."

Guild flicked an eye at Lestrade, who was writing again in his pad.

"You said 'she,'" Lestrade muttered casually. "Got a name?"

Nice try. "Like I said. A client. No name."

"The same one who picked you up later?" Guild put in.

I pointed at Lestrade's pad. "You can write that one down as another 'no comment.'"

"Play it your way," Guild said.

The coroner came huffing up the trail, coat and hat in one hand, the other holding a handkerchief to the back of his head. Although the morning air was warming in the sun, it wasn't nearly hot, but he was a fat man, and the effort of the climb made his face beam red above his bursting white shirt like a cherry on a vanilla ice cream cone.

"Hello, Guild," he puffed. "Lestrade. You fellows seen the bodies yet?"

"Nah, we just got here."

"No problem. They waited for you."

The fat man laughed, but Guild didn't get it. He squinted down into the canyon.

"Who, the Inspector?"

"The bodies, Guild. The bodies waited."

He laughed again, and Guild and Lestrade feebly joined in. The coroner waved his damp handkerchief in my direction.

"This the fellow belongs to the Packard?"

"Yeah, this is him," Guild said.

"Looks like you got some explaining to do," he said jovially. "Top o' the mornin', boys."

"You're not leaving, are you?"

"Why not? I got all I need. Besides, it's past my breakfast."

"But we just got here."

"Yeah, what if we got questions?"

"Talk to the Inspector. I'm done." He mopped his glowing brow—which did indeed look as done as a Sunday ham—and waddled away.

"What about me?" I said to Guild. "Am I done?"

"Not nearly. Come on."

We made our way down the trail to the crime scene. It didn't seem nearly so far from the road in the morning light as it had in the darkness of a few hours before. Fanned out through the brush were two rumpled suits and four uniforms, picking their way around, making a good show, at least, of looking for evidence. A squatting photographer moved in crab-steps around the body of Guy Pollone, popping off one flash bulb after another. Observing disinterestedly were two guys who could have passed for milkmen in their white jackets and caps—except for the folded stretcher propped between them. The morgue boys. Between them and the body was the Inspector, a faceless man in a featureless coat, who hung over Freddy Fergus like a dark, unhappy cloud.

"Whatsamatter, Inspector?" Guild called. "Yer lookin' at that stiff like he owed you money."

The Inspector shifted his gray shoulders, gave a bare rumble of recognition. "It don't figure," he said.

"What don't figure?"

He gestured at the two lifeless bodies, each with its feet pointed toward the other, about twenty feet apart. "Two stiffs, two guns. This one," he said, pointing at Freddy. "He's got a thirty-eight. The other one's got a forty-five."

"So?"

"So, that fellow over there's got a thirty-eight slug in his throat, just like you'd expect. But this fellow..."

He leaned over Freddy and pulled back his jacket to reveal the fist-sized hole in his chest.

"Looks like a forty-five to me," Lestrade said.

"Sure. So far, so good. But what does that look like?"

He pointed to the third eye in Freddy's forehead, a pinky-sized hole of congealed red.

"That can't be anything bigger than a thirty-eight," Guild said.

"That's how I see it. Execution style, right where he lays." He traced in the air the circle of blood-spattered dirt, like hell's halo around Freddy's head.

Guild's brow wrinkled with mental effort. "So, that means we got a third shooter?"

"Either that, or this one was so despondent at being shot in the chest he committed suicide."

Guild nodded sagely. "So, you got an I.D.?"

"Frederick Y. Fergus, Esquire."

"A shyster?"

"Yeah. An expensive one, too, it looks like. Beverly Hills address."

"What about the other one?"

We walked over to have a look.

"Guy Pollone. No details yet, but he's got a license to carry."

Guild looked at me. "One of yours?"

"One of my what?"

"You know," he said with a leer. "Private investigator."

"How should I know? I'd try the secret handshake, but I don't think he's up to it."

"Wise guy," Lestrade said, by way of explanation, to the Inspector.

"Yeah?" The nondescript face looked me over. "I've known a few wise guys. They usually wind up like these stiffs." He nodded up the trail. "So that's his car?"

Guild said, "It's his, all right."

"Got an explanation?"

"Stolen. So he says."

"You believe him?"

"Maybe."

"Except it seems kinda funny," Lestrade put in. We waited for the payoff. "Usually, you steal a getaway car, you use it to get away. Usually."

"Maybe it was this guy that swiped it," I said, pointing at the body. "What'd you say his name was?"

"Pollone," the Inspector said. "Maybe. Except we found his car at the other end of the canyon."

I should have kept my mouth shut. They all eyed me for several uncomfortable seconds.

"Maybe now yer gonna say the shyster swiped it?" Guild said dryly.

"Before you do," the Inspector put in, "you might like to know we found his car in an empty lot at Laurel Canyon and Mulholland."

When I didn't answer, their interest returned to the stiffs.

"So whatta we got, then?" Guild asked.

"Looks like a deal gone bad. Maybe some kind of high-dollar stolen goods. Maybe blackmail."

Three guesses, three cigars. I had to admit, this guy was pretty good.

He pointed at Fergus. "This one musta had a partner. I figure the partner meets him in the stolen car, brings him down here, gets whatever he's after, then..."

He pointed a finger and made the motion of a falling hammer with his thumb.

"The old double-cross," Guild concluded.

"But why steal a car for a job like this?" Lestrade said.

"Yeah," the Inspector said, looking me over again. "That's a good question."

"Inspector! Hey, Inspector!"

One of the uniforms was waving from off in the brush.

"Whattya got?" the Inspector called.

"Shell casings. Twenty-five caliber."

"Flag 'em and leave 'em. I'll have a look in a minute." He turned to Guild. "That makes five."

"Five what?"

"Five shooters. We found some casings from a forty-five automatic just up the hill. Add that to the twenty-five caliber, our two stiffs, and our mystery thirty-eight."

"Musta been like the fourth of July out here."

I could have concurred with Lestrade's description, but I kept my counsel. The forty-five sounded like serious muscle. Maybe the Dominos, maybe some other hired gun. My first thought had been that one of Geiger's boys had brought my piece to the party, but if they had, they would have left it to incriminate me. Or maybe they figured they didn't need to, since they'd left me on the scene to incriminate myself. The twenty-five caliber rang a bell. A woman's gun, just about the size of the one Inez Ravenswood had held to my kneecap.

"Say," Guild said to me, his brow practically steaming from its fevered thoughts. "Don't you have a thirty-eight?"

"I have exactly one Colt forty-five automatic, army issue, registered with the Los Angeles County Sheriff's Department."

"And you couldn't possibly have anything unregistered on the side, you're such a stickler for the rules."

"That one at my office is just for show."

"What's he talking about?" the Inspector wanted to know.

"When we picked him up we found an old Civil War cannon fixed under his desk," Lestrade explained. "Cute setup. Blow the back out of anybody sittin' on the wrong end."

"You looking to get your license suspended, wise guy?"

"It's an antique. Like I said, strictly for show."

"So he doesn't have a thirty-eight," Lestrade said. "Maybe that's his forty-five, up on the hill."

"Maybe, but that still leaves me out of it. It was stolen with my car."

"Why'd you leave it in your car?" Guild growled. "You got a holster."

"So *not* carrying a gun is a crime now?"

Guild got in my face. "You can be *too* funny, you know."

"Take it easy, Guild," the Inspector said, pulling him and Lestrade aside.

They conferred for a couple minutes, muttering and throwing glances my way. I was able to catch some of it. The rest I could fill in. The subject was me and what they had on me, which I gathered was not much. What I knew was that they had a body with a thirty-eight slug that belonged to me, but no gun to match it with. If the forty-five casings they'd found matched the gun Geiger had taken, that could come back to haunt me, but since it didn't look like any of those slugs had wound up inside anybody, I could probably rest easy. Someone had tipped them to the shooting, that was for sure, but they'd probably banked on the cops finding me there with the corpse, gun in hand, and weren't likely to come forward personally and finger me. So that left the cops with only one piece of evidence against me—my car. But as the lab coat had said, the Packard was clean. "A little too clean," I heard Guild grumble. Maybe, but clean nonetheless, and they can't arrest you for that. The only thing they could book me for was the Colt Dragoons, which, technically, as a licensed investigator I should have registered, but, like the now disposed-of thirty-eight, had not. Chalk it up to sloppy bookkeeping. They'd confiscated it, but I could probably get it back by paying a fine.

So I wasn't surprised when they ushered me back up the hill and said I could go, nor even too surprised when they let me take my car. It's my nature to press my luck, though, and I couldn't resist asking if they were filing my stolen car report.

"Sure," Guild said. "And maybe we should hold it down at the impound lot for evidence."

"I love you, too," I said, ducking into the Packard before he could take a swipe at me.

-13-

Except for that brief nap in the canyon, I hadn't seen the backs of my eyelids in almost twenty-four hours. It had been a long day, and an even longer night, but if I wanted a look at Guy Pollone's place before the cops got there—and I did—sleep would have to wait.

I'd gotten the address off Pollone's I.D., and I raced there as fast as morning traffic would allow. For all I knew, L.A.P.D. already had the place locked up tighter than Dick's hat band, so it was a roll of the dice at best, an invitation to arrest at worst. Still, I figured it was worth a shot.

The address was Shetland Lane in Brentwood Heights—about two miles and a million dollars from the Ravenswood estate. A cottage of cracking stucco with a mossy, terra cotta roof, it was set back from the street, almost invisible behind a wall of fragrant oleander. A wildly overgrown trellis clung to one side. The yard was patchy and leaf-strewn, its sole ornament an iron birdbath that was yielding to rust. The whole place had an air of decadence and eccentricity, conjuring images of reclusive old maids, too many cats, and maybe an embroidered hatbox full of stock certificates with names like Standard Oil and Union Pacific. Not the kind of place I'd associate with a fortyish fixit-man with a millionaire for a boss and a blackmailing jazz singer for a partner. I wondered if I checked the County Registry whose name I'd turn up on the deed. My money was on a Ravenswood—but which one?

There was no sign of the cops, so I let myself in the front door. Not an old maid or a cat in sight, but if the exterior of the place was decadent, the interior was downright outré. The alcove was hung with a wall carving of naked Hindus, their vividly depicted anatomy a jigsaw puzzle of interlocking parts. In one corner was an elephant's foot umbrella stand adorned with a fan of peacock feathers. Down three tile steps was a sunken room that could have served as Fu Manchu's opium den—all beads, tapestries, and lacquered wood. A carved Buddha sat before a painted silk screen, smiling serenely down on a lush divan that sat opposite an octagonal, dragon-footed coffee table. The only light in the room came from a line of small, square windows at the top of one wall, giving one an eye-level view of the walk at the side of the house. The place reeked of Saturday night's perfume, booze, and funny cigarettes.

I wrapped a handkerchief around one hand to prevent finger prints and gently ransacked the place, opening up drawers, chests, and what seemed like a hundred little lacquered boxes. Any stimulant or drug you could want—legal or illegal—was there. I found enough booze to start my own pub and enough dope to stay high for a year, not to mention a small library of "artistic" photos and etchings. But not much else—no weapons, no papers, no satchels of money, no jewel-encrusted ram's horn.

I did find one thing, though. Tucked inside a gold-embossed book of erotic poetry was an innocuous-looking piece of folded paper. I unfolded it once, twice. The rough, able hand was familiar, but the subject was new. Instead of a hapless, trapped little man, it was the face of an Egyptian-eyed beauty, her hair piled high in dark ringlets and adorned with a wild, voracious-looking flower. Scrawled at a diagonal across the bottom and punctuated with a dagger-like exclamation point was the name "Dahlia!" just like the poster outside Geiger's club.

I refolded the paper and pocketed it. The cops could show any minute, and I had no time to waste. I pushed my way through a heavy, beaded curtain into a small hallway with three more curtains. I chose the beads to the right and found myself in the kitchen.

If this really was Guy Pollone's house, he wasn't much of a homebody. The floor had a sticky feel and the counter tops were covered with a patina of dust and grunge. The icebox contained a nearly empty bottle of what used to be milk and a mummified piece of cheese that was so dry even mold couldn't grow on it. I shut the door quickly to squelch the sour smell of rotting curds. Except for a few dusty tins of sardines and a box of crackers, the cupboard was empty, too. The only signs of recent life were the empty bottles of booze and the dirty glasses in the sink, but whether they'd been there for a day or a week, I couldn't say.

I opened a drawer and found, stashed among the knives, spoons, and forks, a palm-sized, nickel-plated pistol. My thinking may not have been clear, but it was quick. I stuffed it in my pocket.

That's when I heard the click of the front door latch. I dashed through two sets of beads, burst into the parlor, and came to a dead stop when I barked my shin against the coffee table. Falling to one knee, I managed, thanks to the little square windows, to get my one glimpse of the intruder: two shapely, silk-stockinged legs, running up the walk. I limped to the door. Behind the house, another wall of oleander obscured a figure running up an alley to a parked car. There was the slam of a door, the roar of an engine, the screech of tires. By the time I made it to the alley, there was nothing to see but dust.

I hobbled back to the house, rubbing my shin and cursing myself for my carelessness. I hadn't checked the alley, hadn't checked the rest of the house, hadn't done any of the basics of detective work or just plain common sense. So, either Hellen Vergos or Inez Ravenswood had gotten here ahead of me, heard me breaking in, and hidden herself in the back. I counted myself lucky. If it had been one of Geiger's boys, or some other thug that was more muscle than brains, I might be dead right now.

Had she—whichever she she was—found what she'd come for? I didn't know, but for the moment I had to bet she hadn't. That hope might be all I could salvage from this mess.

My plan had been to get in and get out, learning what I could and leaving the place just as I had found it. The light of day that spilled in through the open door as I reentered the place showed the results of that plan: at the bottom of the tile steps, gazing up at me in serene repose, was the face of the carved Buddha. Three feet away, next to the stand I had apparently jostled during my dance of pain with the cracked shin, lay the statue's other ninety percent.

I uttered a few choice comments on my own intelligence and lineage and pulled the door shut behind me. The statue was in pieces, but it didn't appear to be broken. The Buddha's face had popped off very neatly, and the edges of the ceramic were smooth and regular in my hand. When I hefted the rest of the sculpture back onto its stand it felt surprisingly light, and I saw that it was hollow. Also, there seemed to be a wire running out the back of it, which must have been pretty handy if one wanted to operate the camera I found mounted inside the head. The lens was small, and when the face was re-fastened, it fit neatly within the Enlightened One's open-mouth smile. I followed the wire behind the screen, which seemed to be flush against the wall but actually covered a niche just large enough for a man to sit on the squat, little stool that had been placed there. There was also a peephole through the screen at eye level with the stool, and at the end of the wire a plunger. I pressed the plunger and was dazzled by the flash of a bulb from a specially mounted lamp. It was a sweet setup for a blackmailer. Sex to lure the mark, booze to soften him up, dope to finish him off. Then it's watch the little birdie. I wondered how stoned the mark would have to be not to notice that flash.

But something didn't jibe. If this was the setup that had snared Col. Ravenswood, that would mean the blackmailers had been running the same racket out of the same location for something like twenty years. That didn't seem plausible. In my mind's eye I tried to match the photos of Dahlia and the Colonel I'd seen at the canyon with the setup here. My memory of them was fuzzy, at best, but they seemed different, somehow. Besides, if the blackmailers had the goods on Ravenswood twenty years ago, why wait until now to come out with it?

But maybe it hadn't started out as blackmail. Maybe it had started out as something else. I wondered how long Guy Pollone had worked for the Colonel. If he'd been there when the Colonel had set up his little love nest with the jazz singer—whether it was here or somewhere else—maybe Pollone had felt the need to make a record for posterity. Most fixers and strong-arm men lucky enough to hitch their wagons to a gravy train like Col. Ravenswood figure they're set for life, but a smart operator always hedges his bets. In the private eye racket there's a fine line between getting the goods *for* a client and getting the goods *on* a client, and I'd known plenty who'd crossed that line. Guy Pollone wouldn't be the first keeper of the flame to turn blackmailer.

Checking my watch, I saw that I'd been on the scene for over thirty minutes. That was pushing it, even for L.A.P.D. I pushed the screen back against the wall and fixed the Buddha up good as new, being sure to wipe down with my handkerchief everything I might have touched. I even remembered to go back into the kitchen and close the drawer I'd opened. The pistol I kept.

-14-

I found a phone booth and dialed Hellen Vergos' apartment. No answer. It figured. After I'd spilled it to her about Guy Pollone being shot, it probably hadn't taken her long to realize that whatever he'd had that everyone was after might still be at his house. I thought of going over and surprising her, even breaking in if she didn't show, but I was dead on my feet. I headed back to my place to get some sleep.

Only I didn't sleep. Not much, anyway. When I came in I went straight to the bed, shedding my coat and shoes, unhitching my tie, and unpocketing my new cap gun before I flopped onto my back. I felt like sleep would come the instant my head hit the pillow.

But then I saw the little square of paper tucked away in the frosted glass of the overhead light. It was barely visible in the darkened globe, but I knew it was there. What was it this time? A drowning man? A hanged man? A man on the rack? I didn't want to know. I pulled the pillow over my head to block out the morning light creeping through the Venetian blinds and smother the lurid thoughts bouncing inside my head.

Ten minutes limped by. Twenty minutes. Thirty. Who was I kidding? I needed a drink.

I got up and went to the cupboard, leaving the light off. I could sense the little square of paper above me, situated in the frosted globe like the pupil of an eye, looking over my shoulder, staring down my every move. In the cupboard I found some gin and a bottle of cough syrup. The eye disapproved, but I mixed up a favorite cocktail that usually did the trick when I couldn't sleep. It tasted like grandma's deadliest home remedy, but I took my medicine like a good little boy and went back to bed to let the alcohol and codeine do their work.

I must have gone to sleep, because my dreams were haunted by clanging bells and great, staring eyes, their black pupils erupting in mad streams of frightening, inky figures. I tried to fight them off as they flailed at me with their tentacles and piercing, ragged claws.

Pistol shots jolted me awake. No, hammer blows. No, someone pounding on my door. It was Ma Bailey, shouting for me to open up.

I was on the floor, sweat-soaked sheets around my legs. Something had me by the hand. It was the phone cord, wrapped around my fingers and ripped from the wall. My hands were bleeding from several ragged cuts. In the middle of the room was the smashed globe of the overhead light, its scattered shards littered with tiny scraps of torn paper.

"Mr. York!" I'd never heard Ma sound so outdone. "If you don't open this door, I'm calling the police!"

I swept the dislocated phone under the bed, tucked in my shirt, smoothed my hair. It was the best I could do.

When I pulled the door open, the noon sun was so stabbing it nearly staggered me. My eyes squinted tight, rendering Ma a barely visible shadow. Another shadow hovering behind her I pegged for Mr. Tomahto.

"Mr. York!"

"Morning, Ma." That's what I tried to say. My tongue was so thick it came out more like the murmur of a sleeping schnauzer.

"Are you all right?"

"Just a little under the weather," I said.

"Mr. Pendergast said he heard some sort of terrible commotion coming from your room."

Mr. Pendergast was my closest neighbor. He kept parakeets that woke me every morning at first light. I wiped the sweat from my brow with the back of one hand. "Yeah, um, I was—"

"Your hand!"

"Oh." I looked at it stupidly. The smear of congealed blood made it look worse than it was. "Yeah. I was, um, changing a light bulb "

My eyes had adjusted enough that I could make out their skeptical looks. So I opted for the open door policy. Their eyes went wide as I let them see the mess in the middle of the floor.

"I guess I slipped and fell."

"Oh, my."

At the sight of the broken glass I could see the adding machine behind Ma's eyes already calculating the damages. She looked at Mr. Tomahto, who muttered, "Better sweep up glass."

"Yeah," I said, not knowing if he was ordering or offering. "I was just getting it."

"You'll have to pay for that globe," Ma said.

"Sure, sure," I said. I pulled a bill from my pocket and shoved it at her.

"But that's too much!"

"No, keep it. For your trouble."

She showed the twenty to Mr. Tomahto, who uttered a syllable of exclamation.

"Please."

"Well, if you insist."

"Sorry for the disruption."

"Are you sure you're all right? You might've hit your head."

"No, no. Like I said, just a little under the weather, that's all. I'm fine."

"You're so flushed. Do you have a fever?"

She reached up to feel my head, but I jumped back like she'd come at me with a shiv.

"My, but you're jumpy!"

"Sorry."

I think I'd hurt her feelings, but she tried not to show it. "Do you have alcohol?"

I went blank. Was that an accusation?

"For that cut." She nodded at my hand.

"Oh. Yes ma'am. I'm all fixed."

"Have you anything to eat?"

"Ma'am?"

"Do you have soup? You should have some soup."

"Soup. Yes, ma'am. I've got some chicken noodle."

102

"Chicken noodle. That's good for a fever." She and Mr. Tomahto nodded at each other with approval.

"We'll come by later to check on you."

"That's very sweet of you. Thank you."

"'Bye, now."

The problem with the open door policy is sometimes once you've got the thing open you can hardly get it shut.

As bad as the room looked, it didn't take long to set it right. One disheveled bed, one overturned chair. The broken glass was a pain to get up, but after going over the place several times with the broom I seemed to have it. For once, I was grateful not to have a carpet. I took a few minutes to try to piece together the drawing, but the fragments were so small I couldn't make anything out of it. I must have been really out of my head to keep ripping and ripping past the point of turning the thing into confetti. As for the phone, it could be reconnected, but that would have to wait for later.

I splashed some water on my face and washed the blood from my hands. The cuts weren't too bad. Fortunately, I still had enough gin to disinfect them.

After a quick bath and a fresh change of clothes I felt a hundred percent better, but that was still only about fifty percent of all right. Three hours of troubled sleep—if you could call it sleep—weren't nearly enough to recharge the batteries after the night I'd had.

I sat back on the bed, and the inviting softness was like a physical force that drew me downward. Sleep was a sweet promise, but above me the naked bulb that hung from its socket like a gouged eye left me feeling chastened and unworthy. You can sleep, but you'll get no rest, it seemed to say. There was a man still missing and a treasure still unrecovered, two jobs you'd been paid to see through. There was a beautiful young woman who needed your help, even if she hadn't been completely honest with you. There were people dead. There were other people, nasty people, who maybe needed to be put away, people who had tried to put you away and who needed to be taught that you didn't go down so easy. So there was duty, there was reward, there was even satisfaction to be had. Or maybe there was just survival. But beyond all that, there was a puzzle to be solved, a puzzle with some pieces missing, and one of the pieces seemed to be you. Even if you thought you could let it go, it wouldn't let you go, it would keep coming back to you, in a phone call, in a slip of paper, in a whiff of perfume, or worse, from somewhere inside you, from that black space of unconsciousness that seemed more and more to be opening up beneath you. So there you are, caught in the middle, with nothing to do but carry on.

I sat up, got my feet back on the floor, grabbed a Chesterfield and a light from the nightstand. My hands shook as I lit up.

Get a grip, York.

A lungful of nicotine steadied me. I picked up my new gun off the nightstand to check it out. One look and I had to laugh. Even in the gloom of Guy Pollone's kitchen I don't see how I'd missed it. I aimed the pistol at my reflection in the mirror and pulled the trigger. The muzzle flipped up and spit out a perfect blue flame. A cigarette lighter. Well, you can't always choose your friends and you can't always choose your weapons. I stuffed it in my pocket. It might be risky carrying it around, but sometimes even poor company is better than no company at all.

Despite the brightness of the noonday sun, the air was cool and crisp. The Santa Anas had retreated back into the desert and I could almost smell the salt air wafting lazily in from the sea. The fresh air seemed to arouse my stomach, and I wasn't a block from my apartment before it reminded me that I hadn't eaten a thing since the sandwich I had grabbed yesterday on the way to meet Col. Ravenswood.

I stopped at a curbside stand for a couple tamales wrapped in corn shucks and some coffee wrapped in a paper cup. They'd probably make war in my gut before the day was out, but for now they were as satisfying as Grandma's meatloaf.

Having breakfasted, I pulled up to a phone booth. Professional ethics called for a report to Col. Ravenswood on the fiasco of last night, but I told myself I needed to settle this thing with Hellen Vergos first. I dropped in a nickel and dialed. One ring turned into ten. No answer. I retrieved my nickel and thought again of dialing the Colonel, but as much as I disliked giving a client a negative report, I disliked giving him a prematurely negative report even more. It's not that I thought a chat with Hellen Vergos was likely to give me all the answers, but I figured it would at least give me something to tell the Colonel besides, Sorry, but I lost the "very symbol of your wealth and power" and don't have a clue as to where it's gone. Oh, and by the way, I lost your lawyer, too.

But like they say, you can put off paying the piper, but you still gotta face the music. Or words to that effect. So I dialed the Colonel's private number and waited past any reasonable time for an answer. Now, that was strange. You'd think with a hundred-odd lackeys crawling all over the place, somebody could pick up a phone. But since I wasn't too eager to talk to the Colonel anyway, I chalked it up to my good fortune and headed for Hellen Vergos' place.

When I got to the Denmark Arms I decided to play it straight, at least to start with, and went up to the front desk. The day clerk was a little man in a vest and bow tie who sat on a high stool, the morning paper folded on one knee. The way he frowned and gritted his teeth, he was either working on a very tough crossword or chewing on a very tough pencil.

Since he didn't look up, I spoke first: "Morning. Miss Vergos in?"

He looked at me quizzically and pulled the pencil from between his teeth. "No, she stepped out."

"Any idea when?"

"You a friend of hers?"

"Sure, you could say that. She's doing a little bookkeeping for me."

He frowned at me like I was a seven-letter word for misconception. "I didn't get your name."

"York," I said. Hellen wasn't kidding about them being protective of her. "She's not expecting me, but I was in the neighborhood and thought maybe I could save her a trip to the office."

"I didn't know she was working."

"Just some piece work. You know, doing me a favor, picking up a little money on the side. That kind of thing."

"Uh-huh. What line of work you say you were in?"

I was developing an intense urge to tie this guy's ears together. "Laminated aerodynamic widgets," I pronounced, adding a wink for good measure. "Government stuff."

"Uh-huh."

"So, you haven't seen her?"

"She left about an hour ago."

"An hour ago? Are you sure?"

"Yeah, Mac, I'm sure. I been telling time since I was a kid."

"Okay, don't get sore. It's just that I called this morning and she wasn't in. Maybe she went out and came back?"

106

"Couldn't say. I didn't come on duty till eleven."

"Okay, thanks. Tell her I stopped by, will you?"

"I'll do that."

Okay, so what did I learn? I'd already known she wasn't in when I called this morning. Maybe she'd gone to Guy Pollone's, maybe she'd gone for a loaf of bread. Either way, it didn't prove a thing.

I checked the building's side exit, but it was locked from the inside. So the frontal assault was out, and so was the sidal. That left only the tactical.

I went to a fruit stand across the street, bought a couple kumquats, and had the proprietor bag them up. He had a kid sweeping up, about eleven years old, and I asked if I could borrow him for a couple minutes. I gave the kid the kumquats and fifty cents, pointed out the locked door to him, told him to count to a hundred, go up to the door, and knock on it as loud as he could until somebody opened up.

"Then what?" the kid asked.

"Tell the guy who answers you got his kumquats he ordered."

The kid looked at me dubiously. "Did he really order the kumquats?"

"Probably not."

"He ain't gonna like that."

"There's another four bits in it for you if you do it."

"You swear?"

"On my mother's saintly, gray head. Deal?"

"Deal!"

He started counting, and I jaywalked corner-to-corner to the newsstand across from the front entrance of the apartment building. From behind a copy of *True Detective*, I could just make out the desk clerk, still on his perch. Suddenly, he jumped like somebody had goosed him. Even over the traffic, I could hear the kid pounding against the metal door. It sounded like he was using a brick. The clerk threw his paper aside and went to investigate. I was in.

As I crossed the lobby, I could hear the word "kumquats" echoing repeatedly down the corridor.

"What kumquats?"

"The kumquats you wanted!"

"I don't want any kumquats!"

"Then what'd you order these kumquats for if ya didn't want 'em?"

"I tell you, I didn't order any kumquats!"

The kid must have kept it up like that for five minutes. A real pro.

When I came to the door of Hellen's apartment I listened outside for a second, satisfied myself no one was inside, and tried the knob. Locked, but I made quick work of that. One of the advantages of a misspent youth.

The smell of last night's cigarettes still lingered in the air, mingling unpleasantly with a whiff of perfume. Other than that, the place was as clean and bright as a freshly scrubbed girl scout.

Having learned a lesson from my misadventure at Guy Pollone's, the first thing I did was check behind every closed door, including the Murphy bed. There was only the dressing room and bath, both empty, both clean and well ordered.

I didn't have to bother with fingerprints, so my work went quickly. As searches go, it wasn't much of a challenge—everything neat, everything ordered, everything in its place. Open any drawer, any cabinet, and everything in it was in plain sight. I didn't have to dig through anything, not even the trash, which had been emptied.

There wasn't much in the way of what you'd call personal stuff— no letters or old papers—and the only cash I found was a sugar bowl half-filled with change. In one drawer there was an antique Greek Orthodox rosary she'd probably gotten for her First Communion. There were some pictures, too. A couple more of the Vergoses and one, a little postage stamp of a thing, probably from an old Brownie camera, of Hellen and me as kids. I didn't recognize myself at first—gangly in short pants, my face still childishly round, my mop of hair sun-bleached, almost blond, and a big, gap-toothed smile. I must have been about fourteen, Hellen maybe half that. I was playing big brother, sitting on somebody's stoop and holding Hellen on my knee. In contrast to my beaming face, her brow was a dark, straight line, her mouth a pouty frown, as if she couldn't wait for the picture to be finished. Probably, she thought she was too grown up to be handled like a baby.

A queer sensation came over me. I had an urge to tuck the photo in my wallet, to secrete it away in that misty place where a select trove of childhood memories can be recalled, willingly and uncritically, to be replayed again and again, like the remembered bits of a favorite song. Then a pang, like a phantom twinge of pain caused in one part of the body by an injury to another, rendered the emotion physical, and I dropped the photo as if it had burst into flame.

Why was she lying to me?

Then I found another photo, a program actually, from Geiger's club, a glossy, full-color, promotional spread featuring "Hollywood's Jazz Sensation: Dahlia!" For the first time, I saw Hellen in her mother's face: the exotic eyes, the full lips, the flawless skin that was more *cafe au lait* than olive. But Hellen's brow was different, the dark lines over her eyes fuller, her chin stronger, her nose more her father's—long, classical, but with the slightest flare at the nostrils. Her image came so vividly to mind I felt another pang, this one of self-consciousness, as if she were standing there, frowning down on me, outraged at my intrusion.

I closed that drawer and opened another. Hellen's bank book. I rifled through it, again feeling crummy, but managing to tamp it down. Going back two years was a deposit of five thousand dollars. Probably what her adoptive parents had left her. It had dwindled steadily ever since, showing a few too many payments to Bullock's and select boutiques. Interspersed with the withdrawals were weekly deposits of forty-five dollars, probably her salary from Col. Ravenswood. Not bad for a kid her age, I guess, but it didn't exactly make the Colonel out to be Diamond Jim. The deposits ended, I noticed, three weeks ago, and her bank account was in need of a serious influx of cash. That hundred she had laid on me when she hired me was a serious investment. But what had she hoped to get for it?

The dressing room was a negative, but the designer ensembles, hats, and other frou-frous certainly explained the payments to Bullock's. The Murphy bed held no secrets, nor was there anything behind the mirrors or the pictures on the walls. I was about to call it quits, but as I surveyed the place one last time there was something that bothered me. It was the credenza. I had searched its drawers and come up empty, but the thing just didn't look right. Why didn't the drawers go all the way to the top?

I removed the gold-framed photo, the atomizer, the ashtray and pulled up on the top. It was a hinged lid. I lifted it until it snapped into place like the top of a desk. In fact, it could have very well served as a desk, since the shallow compartment inside was full of writing utensils and stationary. But what caught my eye was a square of paper, not folded this time. Depicted on it, in heavy, black ink, was a pig on a spit, just on the verge of being consumed by fire. There were other drawings, all in the same familiar, rough but able hand, all depicting men and various other creatures being skewered or threatened in some way. There was a pad, too, half of its pages covered with doodles of daggers, black widows, devouring mouths, and leprous-looking flowers. Some depicted nothing but odd swirls, like pinwheels or the gizmos mad doctors in the movies use to hypnotize their victims. The last one I found was of a man's face, his mouth gaping, his eyes two blank swirls, but not so much like pinwheels, the curve subtler, like that of a chambered nautilus. Or maybe even a ram's horn. I pulled the folded drawing of Dahlia out of my wallet, checked the style against the drawings in the credenza, the pose against the photo on the program. A match both times.

I still couldn't figure what the game was. Why hire someone to help you and then do everything you can to trip him up? Why play cheap little tricks on him, keep him looking over his shoulder, even make him question his own good judgment? I couldn't make sense of it, but now I knew one thing, at least. Now I knew the answer to the question that had been nagging me since Hellen Vergos first showed at my office: Friend or foe?

-16-

After leaving Hellen Vergos' apartment, and paying the kid at the fruit stand for a job well done, I headed back toward Gower. But I didn't see any point in going back to my office. Instead, I steered the Packard south, toward that part of Los Angeles known as Dark Town. Thanks to the Domino brothers, my conversation last night with Miss Dahlia hadn't been very satisfactory, and I thought I might have better luck with her in her native habitat.

I took the scenic route, lighting up a Chesterfield as I turned up the part of West Adams known as Sugar Hill. West Adams had some of the oldest, biggest, and most beautiful homes in Los Angeles, places that put a lot of the movie stars' homes in Beverly Hills to shame. Not only were they beautiful to look at, but I always got a kick out of the idea that these mansions that once housed the founding families of the empire were now all owned by blacks. The street had its own movie stars, too, like Stepin Fetchit and Hattie McDaniel, who probably had the money to live anywhere they wanted, so long as they didn't cross the Jim Crow line.

I turned down South Central Avenue, arriving after a few blocks at the Hotel Dunbar. Of the city's hotels that catered to a Negro clientele, it was the swankiest, right in the center of the jazz district, and a hot hangout for musicians since the twenties. In fact, right next door was the old Club Alabam, once my mother's preferred destination for slumming with her underage son, where we had seen all the greats, from Duke Ellington to Lady Day herself. It was a strange obsession of hers, one that would seize her at odd moments, sometimes long after I had gone to bed and never when my father was at home. She liked jazz—that was obvious from all the records she had—but she never seemed to enjoy herself at a club. She just drank and watched, drank and watched, as if she was waiting for the cops to come raid the place. Seeing it again brought a flood of memories—and a queasy feeling to my stomach.

At street level, the Dunbar was all gray stone and classical arches, pretty elegant, but up top just a square, brick box with the odd filigreed balcony here and there. In total contrast to the exterior, the high-ceilinged lobby was done in the Spanish style everybody was so crazy for a few years back: white stucco walls, arched doorways and windows, wrought iron railings along the stairs and mezzanine. The chandeliers, hanging on long chains from the ceiling, were wrought iron, too. Like the neighborhood that surrounded it, the hotel gave the impression of having seen its best days, but it was still nice enough, still the choice spot for the black elite. Even in the middle of the day, the lobby had a club atmosphere, with a hip-looking crowd gathered in one corner around a man noodling on a piano. I didn't know the tune, but the man looked an awful lot like Count Basie.

But I wasn't there to sightsee or take in the local color. I went up to the desk and asked for some stationery, pretended to scribble a note, and stuffed it in an envelope. I wrote Dahlia's name on the outside and handed it to the clerk, a dignified man in pomaded hair.

"I'd like to leave this for Miss Dahlia, please."

"Miss Dahlia, sir?"

"Yeah, the singer. Doesn't she have a suite here?"

"She used to, sir, but it's been some time."

So it looked like finding her room wasn't going to be as easy as the old phony-letter-in-the-cubbyhole trick. "Do you know where she's staying now?"

The clerk put the envelope down on the counter top, his hand resting on it as if ready to slide it back to me. "I believe we have the address, sir. Would you like this forwarded to her?"

I slipped him a fiver. "That's okay. I'll take it myself."

"Very good, sir. You'll find her at the Paisley. Four blocks down."

I could have walked it in seven or eight minutes, but like most Americans these days my feet are made for pedals, not pavement. What with traffic and parking, I drove it in ten.

The Paisley was quite a comedown from the Dunbar, just a pile of sooty bricks slouched on the sidewalk like a sleeping dog It hadn't been much when it was built, and it was even less now. I wondered how it was that a high-dollar chanteuse like Dahlia was living in such a low-rent dump.

I skipped the finesse this time, just stepped up to the grimy desk and asked the grimy clerk where I could find Miss Dahlia. Two bleary, yellowed eyes assessed me, trying to decide what kind of trouble I was.

"Who's asking?"

I dropped a fiver on the ledger. "The Great Emancipator."

He snapped the book shut on the bill as if to trap a scurrying cockroach. "Four flights up. Room six."

I thanked him and mounted a set of stairs that hadn't seen paint since the Reconstruction. Every step moaned and cracked under me in a note between complaint and warning. I felt that every ear in the building must be following my ascent.

The air in the stairwell was ripe and stifling, and by the time I made it to the fourth floor I had my hat off and was using it as a fan. I found the peeling door of number six, knocked, waited, knocked again. A muffled voice said something unintelligible, maybe to me, maybe to no one. Feet shuffled on the floor, the peephole darkened.

Then nothing. I knocked again. "Open up," I said, mimicking the growl of my friend Guild.

The door cracked open, and I got a face full of pistol, a Nazi Luger pointed right at my nose. At the other end was Dahlia, looking like she'd just rolled out of bed.

"So, it's you," she said thickly.

The Luger was steady enough, but the woman behind it looked shaky. Her eyes were unfocused, her pupils dilated. I raised my hands, holding my hat just a moment at her eye level, then dropping it. I never tried this little distraction on a pro, but on an amateur it works every time. Before the hat hit the floor, I had her arm twisted behind her and the gun in my hand. I shoved her through the door and onto the bed. She didn't yell, but I grabbed my hat out of the hallway and shut the door quick, just in case.

The Luger was warm in my hand, like she'd been sleeping with it. I slipped out the magazine and unchambered the money round as she raised herself up on her elbows, her robe falling off one shoulder to reveal a dangerous amount of cleavage.

"Why, grandma, what big...bullets you have."

She pulled her robe closed, but her expression was anything but demure. "Whaddya want?"

Instead of answering I gave the room the once-over. It was cramped, cluttered, looking more like a dressing room than an apartment, with the wigs, costumes, and under things scattered about. A vase of her signature flowers was wilting on the radiator. I wondered again how a star like Dahlia had come down to this. Then my eye lit on the syringe.

"You're no cop," she said.

"That's right. But you're repeating yourself."

"Well, if you're not a cop, then get the hell outta my place."

I ignored that. "Your friend Guy Pollone is dead."

If she felt surprise, it barely registered. "That figures. I told him he was in over his head."

"Freddy Fergus, too."

Nothing.

I started poking around the room, keeping one eye on Dahlia as she watched me.

"Make yourself to home."

The overflowing ashtrays, empty gin bottles, and used syringes spoke eloquently of a life on the skids. The publicity photos on the walls—of Dahlia with Bob Hope, Joe DiMaggio, Cab Calloway— spoke of a career that, in another place and time, might have gone straight to the top. The photos, the notices, the programs—it was all the usual show business stuff, except that instead of putting it all in a scrapbook, she'd tacked it up on the walls, maybe as a reminder of who she was, or, like Ma Bailey's shrine to herself, who she used to be.

Ironically, it was Dahlia's mirrored vanity that showed the heart that beat beneath the glitter. Among the clutter of combs, brushes, powder puffs, and atomizers was a hinged photo frame. In the frame on the left was a photo of Dahlia, peering wistfully into space. In the frame on the right, as if it were the object of the other photo's longing gaze, was Hellen Vergos, her image as perfect and aloof as a marble sculpture. Other photos of Hellen—as a child, as a bobby-soxer, as a high school graduate—were arranged in a rainbow around the mirror, making Dahlia's vanity not a shrine to herself, but to the daughter she had birthed and lost long ago. In none of the photos, I noticed, were Hellen and Dahlia pictured together.

Once upon a time, a young girl got in a tight spot and made a deal with the devil. After a lifetime of regrets, she wanted a new deal, only maybe nobody was buying, so she decided to get tough. Only you don't get tough with the devil, so somebody winds up dead, and now she can't sleep at night without a hit of junk and a cold piece of steel to cuddle up with.

I picked up the hinged photo frame, pretended to look at it. I needed to get back to business before I started feeling sorry for her.

"They say a picture's worth a thousand words," I said. "Or is that a hundred thousand G's?"

"Pictures," she sneered. "I got something worth a lot more than that."

"The ram's horn."

She smiled at me like I was someone's lost, idiot child.

"They're a dime a dozen, but one's worth a million."

"What's that, some kind of riddle?"

"Somebody tried to make sure they don't have any more, but I got one, the one and only."

"Talk sense!"

"Go to the courthouse, if you don't believe me. They'll set you straight."

"What are you talking about? The place on Shetland Lane?"

She looked at me foggily.

"Whose name's on the deed?" I demanded, taking a step toward her.

She laughed. "You're lost, baby. Lost, lost, baby…"

Her words were getting thick again. I pulled her up from the bed, holding her by the shoulders.

"Where is it? You know what I'm talking about."

"Lost, baby. Lost, lost, and you'll never find your way…"

"The ram's horn! Where is it!" I shook her, but her face just held that stupid, junkie grin, her head lolling back and forth as if on a spring.

"Ahh, what's the use!"

I shoved her back on the bed, determined now to tear the place apart if I had to.

"I got my ticket, baby," she said, as I began ransacking the drawers of her vanity. I doubted I'd find the dingus here, but there had to be a claim check, a safety deposit key, something.

"Yeah, I got mine. I figure it's worth 'bout half of everything old man Ravenswood had."

I knew she was stoned half out of her head, but there was something in her voice that stopped me.

"Had? Whattya mean, 'had'?"

"Ain't you heard, baby? Old Ravey-boy's dead."

They weren't so welcoming at the Ravenswood place this time, but I saved them the embarrassment of turning me away.

When the guard at the front gate held up a hand to stop me, I hit the gas. He had the good sense to get out of the way.

At the end of the gravel drive, I skidded the Packard to a stop behind an *Essex*-class limousine being loaded by a team of valets with trunks, hatboxes, and portmanteaus. I didn't see Jeffers among them, and I didn't wait around to be greeted by one of his expert judo flips.

I bounded up the steps of the mansion and entered the wide-open double doors, pushing past several surprised servants. The entry hall was as spacious as a French cathedral, bustling with maids and butlers pushing and pulling things about, rolling things up, covering other things with sheets. It looked like the place was about to be closed up for an extended vacancy.

I spotted Inez, dressed for travel, supervising from the top of a riser. Someone behind me shouted, "There he is!" and Inez turned in time to see me get manhandled by a couple of beefy Ravenswood employees.

She smiled, enjoying the show a minute before she spoke.

"It's all right, boys. Mr. York is a guest."

"York?"

One of the guards brandished a clipboard, ran his finger down a column. "But he's not on the list, ma'am."

"That's fine. I'll take care of him."

I looked at the guards. They looked at each other.

"Whatever you say, ma'am."

They reluctantly let me go, warning me with their eyes that I'd better not get out of line.

"We'll be right outside, ma'am."

Looking down on me from the riser, Inez let the guards make their exit before she spoke. "I see you've heard the news."

"When did it happen?"

"It was quite sudden. The doctors say it was heart failure."

She took a long, bored drag from an onyx cigarette holder. What a piece of work she was. Standing in the webwork light of a stained glass window, her hair a shimmering halo, her body a wasp's silhouette, she was a living jewel, cold, hard, and mesmerizing.

"You know, you're beautiful when you're in mourning."

She exhaled a listless cloud of nicotine and descended several measured steps to my level.

"It's no secret that our marriage for some time had been a mere formality."

No secret, but her voice was barely audible above the hubbub in the room.

"And now you're cashing in."

"You'd be surprised. Some men carry their bitterness beyond the grave."

I let that one sink in. Then my old friend Jeffers came down the steps, carrying two suitcases. His eyes cut the barest look at me as she stopped him.

"Are those his things?"

"Yes, M'um."

"Is that all?"

"The young lady is packing the rest, M'um."

"I told you not to leave her up there alone!"

"Begging your pardon, M'um, but—" He made as if to put down the two suitcases. "Shall I—"

"Never mind. Put those in the car."

"Yes, M'um." Another quick cut of his eyes before he made a servile, un-military turn on his heel. The jaunty ex-commando of yesterday was gone, replaced by a glorified bellhop.

"Looks like you're going on a trip," I observed.

"Well!" Inez said in a gush of sarcasm. "It's just one brilliant deduction after another, isn't it? As a matter of fact, I'm taking a cruise. Don't bother to see me off."

"Who's your travel companion?"

Her answer was a smug smile.

"A secret, huh? Maybe I should ask the young lady upstairs."

"Maybe you should see yourself out. Or I could call Max and Henry back to show you out."

"I think I can find the way." I tipped my hat to her.

"Good day, then."

She turned and disappeared through a set of sliding doors, not bothering to see that I really left. Her mistake. I thought if I poked around for a minute among the servants, asked a few questions, maybe I could learn a thing or two before I was tossed out. Then I heard someone hissing at me from the top of the stairs.

"Psst! York! Up here!"

It was Hellen Vergos, her stage whisper getting the attention of every servant in the hall. But no one made a move to interfere, so I went on up.

When I got to the top, the whispering resumed.

"What are you doing here?" It sounded like an accusation.

"I might ask you the same."

She gave a thoughtful nod. "We can't talk here. Come on."

She turned and led me around the balcony. It encircled three sides of the entrance hall and was lined with heavy, carved doors. I followed two paces behind, watched her heels pump like pistons on the carpeted floor.

"Tough news about the Colonel."

Her head turned just sideways as she kept walking. "Yes."

"I got the news from an interesting source. A junkie jazz singer who claims to be your mother."

That put a hitch in her step, but she didn't answer. She stopped at a door, opened it. "In here."

I followed her in, shut the door behind us. It was a bedroom but a strange bedroom, the walls completely papered over with movie posters and lobby cards. Tough-guy stuff, mostly, with lots of leggy dames and smoking guns and the brooding eyes of Bogart, Raft,

Robinson, and Ladd looking hard under snap brim fedoras. The bookshelves were crammed full of everything from pulp titles, like *True Crime* and *Black Mask*, to highbrow stuff like *The Complete Works of William Shakespeare*, and the floor was scattered with more books and magazines and stacks of film canisters. In one corner was a 16 mm projector, in another a fold-up movie screen. Amidst all the junk, the four-poster bed looked out of place. The matching dresser fit, though—its mirror was like the walls, almost completely plastered over with lobby cards and pix ripped out of *Photoplay* magazine. There was a half-filled suitcase splayed out on the bed, and many of the dresser drawers stood open.

Hellen stood with her back against one heavily curtained window, eyeing me as if she might at any moment jump out of it.

"Dahlia used to work in the kitchen at the Colonel's country club," she began. "He heard her singing one day. That's how she got his attention. She was just a teenager, but...they became lovers. He put her up in a house he owned, kept her dependent on him. Just money, at first. Then drugs. When I was born, the Colonel made Dahlia give me up. His housekeeper, the woman I always knew as my mother, helped with the birth. She didn't have any children, so she and her husband took me in as their own. They never told me."

"How'd you find out?"

"Some of the details I got later, from Dahlia. The rest of it...The Colonel threw it all in Hammie's face. He was so cruel." She frowned with remembering. "No. Not cruel. Indifferent. It had nothing to do with me. He told it all, with me standing there, as if I wasn't living flesh and blood. His flesh and blood."

She waited for me to speak, but I had nothing to say. Her eyes grew liquid, bitter.

"The poor, little dark-eyed Greek girl," she said. "The immigrant maid's child. Isn't that a riot?"

She laughed in a way that showed she thought it was anything but funny. I decided to change the subject.

"So, what are you doing here?"

She wiped her eyes with both hands in one swift motion. "This is Hammie's room. I'm looking for some clue as to where he might be."

120

I gestured at the posters on the walls. "Have you checked the movie houses?"

"This is no time for jokes."

"So who's joking?"

I noticed a book on the nightstand and idly picked it up. A page was marked with a folded scrap of paper. I opened the book, unfolded the paper. It was a photo spread of Keystone's Bathing Beauties that I recognized from Ma Bailey's collection. Eight girls sitting on the edge of a boat, each with her fingers clasped around one raised knee. Pretty racy stuff for the time. But one of the girl's faces was inked out so thoroughly it looked like a hole into another dimension. I stared at the picture, trying to remember which one was Ma.

"What is it?" Hellen asked.

I held up the book for her to see. The margins were full of scribbled notes and several passages were heavily underlined. I read one, diverting Hellen's attention as I pocketed the photo:

> "The ram vaulted into the air with Helle and Phryxus on his back, till when crossing the strait that divides Europe and Asia, the girl fell into the sea, which from her was called the Hellespont."

I snapped the book shut and read the cover: *Bullfinch's Mythology*. "This guy must be murder at cocktail parties."

"Hammie has lived most of his life in books and movies," she said. Her tone was neither defensive nor critical. Just the facts.

"So what does it mean?"

She didn't answer. Instead, she went to the dresser, pulled open another drawer.

"All right. Then tell me what's going on. How'd you get in here?"

"I'm living here now. Or will be. The Colonel's will stipulates a room and small allowance for me as long as I want it."

I pushed my hat back on my head. "You ladies move fast. How'd you get a copy of the will?"

"Inez. She showed it to me."

"That was generous of her."

"You can bet it's not."

She started rifling through the drawer's contents.

"I don't suppose there's any point in asking how Inez got the will."

"Probably not. She's very resourceful."

"So how did she make out?"

"The same arrangement. Everything else goes to Hammie."

I couldn't help laughing. Hellen tried to cover her irritation by rummaging more fiercely through the drawer.

"Well, I'll say one thing for the old man. He had a wicked sense of humor."

Hellen shut the drawer and faced me squarely. "You don't understand. Hammie's in great danger. Inez is sailing on the *LaPaloma* tonight for Acapulco. She means to take Hammie with her."

"What for? To knock him off?"

"Worse. To marry him."

I rattled my head to stop the spinning. "I need to sit down."

I sat. The room was dark and cool, but there was something stifling about it, of ripe celluloid and mildewed paper. Tyrone Power seemed to smirk down at me from *Nightmare Alley*.

"We don't have much time." Hellen went to another drawer, her words racing as fast as her fingers. "That was her plan from the beginning. Inez was Hammie's nurse a few years ago when he was...institutionalized."

"Institutionalized? You mean in a nuthouse?"

"A sanitarium. When Hammie was released, she talked her way into coming here as his live-in nurse."

"With opportunities for advancement."

"She had Hammie wrapped around her little finger. It was only a matter of time before they eloped."

"But then the old man got a load of her and figured he could use a little nursing himself."

Hellen smiled crookedly. "Inez was only too happy to oblige."

"Sure. Why settle for second base when you can knock it out of the park?"

"When the Colonel married Inez, Hammie was devastated. We'd known each other since we were children, when Mother—Mrs. Vergos—would bring me here to play. Sometimes, his mother would drop him off in our neighborhood. Just let him out of her car in the middle of the street. Usually, it was in the evening, and we might not see her again until morning. He was so alone. I was his friend, his comfort. One thing led to another—"

"And then Pops dropped bomb number two."

Hellen straightened from her search, gazed into the single exposed patch of dresser mirror as if it were a door into memory. "Hammie used to worship that man. He was so naive, so innocent."

"Weren't we all."

She shut the drawer. "There's nothing here."

"You've checked the rest of it?"

She nodded.

"No clue where he might be?"

"Geiger's got him. I know that much."

"Geiger?"

"He and Inez have been in this together from the start."

"What's his angle?"

"Geiger's always got an angle. He's got some kind of hold over Inez, or she's got a hold over him. Either way, I think they find it convenient to use each other."

"Just another page in the all-American family album."

"Yeah..."

I stood up. "So. I guess that's it, then."

She looked at me as if I'd burst into an aria from Wagner. "What do you mean?"

"I mean the Colonel had it right from the beginning. Hammie's never been missing. He's a grown man. He can do what he wants."

"But—"

"Look, it's simple. You meet him at the boat. You say your piece. Either he goes or he stays. It's his decision."

"You promised me you'd find him."

"Call the cruise line. They'll tell you just where he's going to be and when. I call that found." Before she could say it, I cut her off.

"Don't worry. I may be shady, but I'm basically honest. You'll get your money back."

I made to leave, but she grabbed me by the coat.

"I don't care about the money!" If there was anger in her voice, it was drowned in panic. "Can't you see I need your help?"

"I can't turn back the clock for you, baby."

"You don't understand. Hammie's completely in their power. Even if he wasn't so suggestible, they've probably got him doped up. For all we know, he's already on the ship, locked up, helpless."

She put her face in my chest. I could feel the tears through my shirt.

"So, this is sisterly love?"

To my tie she said, "It's love. I don't know what kind."

I didn't say anything. She looked up at me with wet, pleading eyes.

"Won't you help me?"

"You haven't played it straight with me from the beginning. What I oughta do is sock you one."

The pleading eyes turned defiant.

"Go ahead. It won't rub off."

I stroked her permanent wave, noticed at the base of her scalp the kinks from a day of neglect.

"Such dark hair..."

"Be mean to me. I don't care."

I put one finger under her chin, tilted her head back.

"Such full lips..."

"Be cruel—be cruel!"

I kissed her. No resistance this time. Her breath was hot, her body one quivering muscle against mine. The room disappeared, and I felt my stomach leave me as I fell down a bottomless shaft.

A sharp rap at the door brought me back, panting into her dark, wet face.

"Miss Vergos?" Jeffers' voice said through the door. "Pardon me, but Madam wishes me to finish the packing."

As I pulled back, her arms tensed around me, but she needn't have bothered. Those Egyptian eyes held me tighter than chains.

"Don't worry, Angel. For you, I'd jump off a cliff."

-18-

By the time I got back to my office, the eastern sky was just turning gray. The "Live Girl-" sign wasn't lit yet, and the letters on the movie marquee were a meaningless jumble being rearranged for the next title.

My office was as cheery as ever, the last rays of sunshine that bled through the Venetian blinds setting every particle of dust in high relief. I sat at my desk, scribbling on a pad, the phone's receiver cocked between my ear and shoulder as I took down the information from the cruise line.

The *LaPaloma* was sailing at midnight. They claimed not to have any information on a Mr. or Mrs. Ravenswood. Maybe they'd been instructed to keep mum or maybe they just didn't know anything. Inez got plenty of mileage on the Ravenswood moniker, so it didn't make sense to me that she would be traveling under an assumed name. But then again, according to Hellen this trip wasn't exactly on the up-and-up. I tried Geiger's name, but didn't have any more luck with that. With all the questions, the clerk was getting suspicious, so my hand was forced. I booked passage for myself and Hellen under the names of Mr. and Mrs. Nick Charles. With no help and no leads, getting on the boat might be our only chance.

But I didn't like it. My line was lost goods, wayward husbands, and prodigal children. Who was I to stand in the way of two consenting adults' wedded bliss?

Rule number one in the detective's handbook is don't get involved with a client, but somewhere along the line my brains had descended to my lower anatomy and the rules went out the window. Supposedly, I was in this to do a job. Well, let's say the job comes off, aces all around, I rescue the rightful heir to the throne and reunite him with the beautiful young princess. And let's say I don't get my ears clipped in the process. What's the payoff? Another fifty bucks, at my usual rates, for a job well done? Maybe a hundred for going above and beyond? Business is business, but I still had nine hundred dollars in my office safe, and what I needed more than another C-note in my collection was a vacation. Acapulco sounded nice, and when I booked passage on the *LaPaloma* I admit I had a moment there where I pictured Hellen Vergos' tanned body lolling in the surf at sunset with me lying beside her sipping tequila from her navel. But then I saw Hammie Ravenswood standing over us in his Harold Lloyd glasses and silk smoking jacket, saying things like "Good show!" and "Pip! Pip!" and I remembered that three's a crowd, and despite a couple tender moments between me and Hellen, compared to His Highness I was about twenty million light, which was likely to make me odd man out. With enough cash on the line, taboos against little things like murder and even incest are apt to seem downright quaint. The problem was, everyone else involved in this penny-dreadful was in it for the money, one way or another, and that's good business, but me, I was in it for the dame, and in my experience, that's a loser every time.

So, that's if the job comes off all right. And what if it didn't come off? In the heat of the moment I'd told Hellen Vergos I'd jump off a cliff for her. But the truth of the matter is I'm allergic to cliffs.

I picked up the phone, listened a moment to the dial tone, tried a couple digits of the number Hellen had given me. I was debating whether to dial the rest of them, wondering what I would say to Hellen when I reached her, when I saw a long, thin shadow fall across the glass of my office door.

The shadow moved stealthily, taking the doorknob and turning it so slowly it made no sound and barely moved. I softly cradled the phone, reached under the desktop for the old Colt, remembered that Guild and Lestrade had confiscated it. Reluctantly, I slid my hand in my pocket and gripped the cigarette lighter. Overhead the light was off, but there was still enough sunlight creeping in through the Venetian blinds to leave me with no shadow to retreat into. I was a sitting duck.

126

The door swung open, and the bright hallway light rendered the tall figure nothing more than a dark outline. He stood in the doorway, peering in, looking right at me, I knew, even though I couldn't see his eyes under his wide-brimmed hat. I sat, frozen, waiting for him to make his move.

The shadow took a halting step forward. Then another. His movements were stiff, unsure. There was something in his hand, something long and round, like the barrel of an enormous gun. He raised it slowly, pointing it right at my chest. I braced myself, ready to duck, to bluff with the toy gun, to lunge for his weapon, even jump out the window.

Then another step, into the blinds' ladder of yellow light. The thing pointed at my chest was a rolled up newspaper. The man holding it was Col. Ravenswood.

He staggered forward, his legs barely working. I gripped the arms of my chair, but I couldn't stand, couldn't speak. He was looking right into my eyes.

His mouth worked as if to speak, but only choked, gurgling sounds came out.

He took another faltering step, braced himself against the side of the desk. The Adam's apple of his long, thin neck bobbed laboriously, and he tried to speak again.

"The—rumors—"

He waved the paper before my face as he groped for the strength to go on.

"Of my—death—are—greatly—exaggerated—"

The last word came out with a long, tubercular rattle, and he sprawled across my desk, his head striking the wooden top with a thud. The paper dropped open into my lap. Dazed, I looked at the big, black letters of the headline:

"FINANCIER H.H. RAVENSWOOD DEAD."

Under that, in smaller type:

"Died peacefully in his sleep after long illness, says young widow."

I stared at the photo next to the headline—or, rather, it stared up at me, the Colonel's penetrating eyes throwing out a challenge from beneath the bushy furrow of his brow. The figure crumpled across my desk looked more like a scarecrow than a man, with only the tip of his long, vulture nose visible beneath the brim of his hat. I was just bold enough to touch the crown, but the thought of being confronted by two sets of those staring eyes stayed my hand from uncovering his face.

"Colonel?" I ventured. "Colonel Ravenswood?"

No response. I got to my feet and checked his pulse. He was dead, all right, but it wasn't from a long illness. A knife was sticking out of his back, its hilt curved in the shape of a ram's horn. Even in the fading twilight, the spiral of jeweled gold was dazzling.

"So you found your treasure after all, old man," I said. "But it cost you."

There was nothing to be done for the old man now but look after his estate. Thinking quickly, or maybe thinking not at all, I unfurled a handkerchief, wrapped it around the hilt of the knife, and pulled it free. Holding it in my hands, I gaped dumbly at the cruel, blood-smeared blade, at the sparkling gems that encrusted the golden hilt like an organic growth. A hundred grand the old man had been willing to pay to get it back, but it must have been worth ten times that. It was the stuff schemes are made of, schemes as garish and wicked as the knife itself.

I placed the dingus on the newspaper, folded it over, my hands working on automatic as my brain raced ahead. When the cops came they'd be very interested in the murder weapon, but my first concern was whoever had misplaced it in Ravenswood's back. They'd be looking for it, too, so I had to move fast.

I pulled on my coat and grabbed my hat. A couple more folds of the newspaper formed a neat package, which I tucked under my arm. I was almost to the door, when the phone rang.

I spun around, cringing back from the ringing phone like I would from a snarling Doberman. The voice I knew was on the other end of the line seemed already to be talking in my ear, sneering at me, laughing at me. But I got a grip on myself. After all, what could he do if I didn't pick up?

No time for chitchat.

I ran out the door and down the steps, not waiting for the elevator. When I hit the lobby I could see that the street was bustling with end-of-the-day traffic—easy to get lost in, but good cover for a tail. The day janitor was standing in the entryway, wearing a rakish hat and smoking a cigarette, waiting to hand the building over to the night guy. He eyeballed the package under my arm.

"Something for the morning mail, Mr. York?"

I answered the question by making like a periscope looking for enemy vessels. "Seen any spooky characters hanging around lately, Sam?"

Sam deadpanned me. "All the time, Mr. York. All the time."

I gave him a look that I hoped conveyed just how much I appreciated his help. I stepped out on the sidewalk, glanced left and right. The Packard was parked nearby, but any number of people could have been watching it—the two suits at the news stand, the leather jacket in the coffee shop window, even the skirt at the bus stop. As if by old habit, my feet carried me across the street to the movie house. Sometimes, if my office got too hot for me, I'd park myself there for a cool, comfortable think. The thermometer at the bank read a balmy seventy-seven, but I gauged the heat I was under at about a hundred and ten.

I fished a coin out of my pocket and asked the girl behind the glass for a ticket. She popped a pink bubble the size of a grapefruit and laid aside a copy of *Cin-o-Grams*, marking her place with her finger. "For tonight?"

"No, now."

"But the matinee's almost over."

"You want the quarter or not?"

She invited me to suit myself, which I did, taking the ticket and handing it off to a pimply usher. I found a seat in the back row, where I could watch all comings and goings. There was hardly anybody in the theater, and I slouched low in my seat to be as inconspicuous as possible. If I wanted to stay healthy I needed to get as much space between me and the package as possible, but I needed a stash where it would be safe and where I could access it—

or where I could get it to the cops if something happened to me. I had an urge to just stuff it under my seat and make for the exit. Judging from the amount of gum my shoes had picked up from the floor, I wouldn't have to worry about a cleaning crew coming through and stumbling over it any time soon.

After five minutes passed with nobody coming in after me, I went from red alert to yellow. The movie was *Andy Hardy's Double Trouble*, I think. Kid stuff, but it brought back memories of me and little Hellen taking in matinees with Mamma Vergos on her days off. What a crew we were—a Greek immigrant, a half-black "love" child, and an aspiring juvenile delinquent, wallowing in the pillowy comfort of America's most all-American family. I remembered how Hellen used to love the Hardy movies, prattling on after each one with keen eight-year-old insight about which girl was Andy's ideal mate. Being older, I sneered at the soppy story lines and corny dialogue—but how many times did I secretly wish for a father like kindly, wise, old Lewis Stone?

I wasn't there to watch a movie—or take a trip down memory lane. My mind was still buzzing with images of the dead millionaire, the jeweled knife, and the rogues' gallery of suspects that might have been zeroing in on me that very minute. But the characters on screen still managed to get a word in.

Says Betsy Booth: "Now, don't you feel glad just to be alive?"

Replies Andy: "I've never before appreciated the advantage of being dead."

I snorted at that, loudly enough that several heads swiveled my way. I hunkered down a little further in my seat, but that only seemed to make the images on screen loom larger above me. That's the thing about the movies, they can make even a couple of pygmies like Mickey Rooney and Judy Garland giants among men. The words they spoke, the music they danced to, and the songs they sang seemed to slide past my ears, but the images pulled me in. The picturesque neighborhood. That perfect house. Those earnest faces. They'd never heard of Hitler. The Depression had passed them by. They'd never seen a problem that couldn't be worked out with a good, honest heart-to-heart and a tall glass of Mom's lemonade.

I must have dozed off, because the next thing I was aware of was the rapping of a flashlight on my seat back.

"Show's over, Mister," the pimply usher was saying.

I muttered some response, got my bearings. "You got a back exit?"

He waved his flashlight toward the screen, where two signs glowed, one on either side.

"Take your pick."

Outside it was dark, with the slightest red glow on the horizon. I couldn't have been in the theater for more than twenty minutes, though it seemed like an hour. I walked the long way around the block to the Packard, a plan formulating in my head. I didn't spot any tail, but taking no chances, I zigged and zagged through the streets downtown to Union Station. If anyone had been on me, by now he was either very lost or very good. I stashed the dingus in a public locker, dropped the key in an envelope, and scribbled a note to Ma Bailey telling her to keep it in a safe place until I came for it. Just to drive home the seriousness of the matter, I added that if she didn't hear from me in a week to contact Lt. Guild of L.A.P.D. She may have been a batty old dame, but she was stubborn as a plow mule, and I knew I could trust her to give the key to me and no one but me.

With the dingus stashed and the key in the mail, I jumped in the Packard and cruised aimlessly through the streets, but generally tacking west. What bothered me about this tangled mess was everything, and it wasn't easy to decide which string to pull next. Had the Colonel's death—the peaceful one described in the newspaper—been a stunt? Was it some kind of diversion to throw off his enemies? Easy to say, but not so easy to get past the papers, not to mention the cops. Unless you owned them, which a guy with the Colonel's juice well might. And how did the dingus wind up in the Colonel's back? Who would kill a guy with the very thing they were supposedly killing him for? Not Geiger, that's for sure, and not the Dominos. They were stupid, but not that stupid. It had to be someone who had more hatred at heart than greed. A betrayed son or daughter, maybe. That made Hammie and Hellen prime candidates. I liked Hammie for the job, but maybe that was just prejudice for all the trouble he was causing me. A spurned lover—that was another possibility. But not Inez. Dahlia was the one who'd convinced me that she had the ram's horn or knew where it was. She was the one who'd told me Ravenswood was dead. And who but a junkie would be crazy enough to leave a million-dollar antique in an old man's back just for a moment of sweet revenge?

I headed down South Central to the Paisley, blew past the desk clerk and up the stairs to Dahlia's apartment. When I got to her door that cold thing gripped me again by the back of the neck. Her door was ajar, light emanating into the hallway from an odd angle, a rhythmic *scritch-scritch* sound gnawing at my ear.

Misplaced chivalry had led me to leave the lady with her gun, so with nothing to protect me but a dime store novelty and a scowl, I pushed the door open.

Whoever had come after me had finished the job I'd started a while before. The place was completely torn apart. The odd-angled light was coming from a lamp on the floor. The *scritch-scritch* was a jazz record spinning on the hi-fi.

At first, I didn't see her. Then I spied a slippered foot under the trash-strewn mattress of her bed. I pulled the mattress aside. There she lay, her tongue protruding from her gaping mouth, her eyes bulging, dead, a strap tight around one arm, the needle still in her vein.

I got out of there, stopping at the desk and telling the clerk as coolly as I could that he needed to call the cops. I laid a fifty on him to make him forget he'd seen me. If he remembered anyway it might go hard for me later, but I had another body to worry about.

By the time I got back to my office building it was well after dark. I made sure I was seen entering the lobby, chatted up the night janitor, asked him if he had the time, just to make sure he'd remember. As far as he was concerned, I was just getting in, and that was the story I wanted him telling the cops.

When I let myself into my office, the first thing I saw was my neatly ordered desk. No body. No blood. No nothing.

The last thing I saw was a big, black anvil aimed straight at my jaw.

-19-

Shadows and fog.

Blurs. Mists. Shapes. Ghost-images.

A bare room. A stinking mattress on an iron bunk. Above, a steel-caged bulb that never goes dark.

Someone in the room. A voice talking through a pillow, muffled and small. A man? A woman? I can't tell. It's muttering, on and on, but I can't make out a single word. Then another voice very clearly says, *Shut up!* The first voice goes quiet. I think it was mine.

A sharp prick in my arm. I try to pull away, but I can't move. Strapped down? Paralyzed? Nausea grips me. I vomit darkness.

Hours pass. Days. Images come to me in an endless dream I can't wake up from: Hellen Vergos, lying on the beach in her schoolgirl clothes, the surf licking at her thighs. Col. Ravenswood, stilt-legged, walking toward me, his hands cradling a strange flower. Or is it Dahlia's head? Singing now, her body floating like an angel above a blue stage. The spotlight shines down, blinding me, now becoming an eye, a third eye in Geiger's forehead. He stands over me, white-smocked, masked, speaking in a language I can't understand, attaching strange instruments to my body. The instruments become a thousand toothy, clawed creatures ripping at my flesh.

I scream. It's dark. Then light again. A stream of inky images pours into the room. The Domino Brothers. They come and go like a recurring nightmare. Punches, kicks, buckets of cold water. Pills poured down my throat, now whole bottles of liquor.

A black cyclops taunts me: *Look at 'im. Boy wouldn't know a hawk from a hound dog.*

Laughter echoes from a whirl of fun-house faces.

Blackness again. An electric jolt brings me awake, strapped to a chair in a dark cell, one brilliant light blinding me, so close I can feel its heat on my face. A disembodied voice, foreign-accented, barks at me repeatedly: *Where—* (or is it *What?*)—*is the ram's horn?* I speak, but I don't recognize my voice or understand my own words. *He's out of his head,* a voice says. Inez Ravenswood's face, like an evil moon, leans in out of the darkness, holding a smoldering butt in a long, silver cigarette holder. Or is it a needle? A huge, spitting syringe. *This won't hurt a bit,* she says, and plunges the smoking needle into my neck.

I scream again, a naked soul plunging into the void. My only marker is that evil moon, retreating a million light years away, until it's a barely visible point in a starless ocean of night, then growing again, larger, closer, but no longer a moon, a clock, its hour hand a dagger approaching midnight.

But not a clock. A human face. Slicked, dark hair. Pencil mustache. Harold Lloyd glasses. Someone talking to me, slapping me across the face.

Wake up. Wake up, Buddy. It's time to get out of here.

My vision is all a blur, but an acrid aroma is vivid in my nostrils. It smells like three days in the Hollywood drunk tank. It smells like me.

Another slap. The blurred face comes back into focus.

That's right, pal. It's your old chum, Hammie, riding in like the cavalry.

He props me up, swings my legs off the bunk. I look down at them, two shriveled stems in dirty, urine-stained pajamas. The naked, bluish feet sticking out at the ends seem alien and far away.

That's it. Let's get you on your feet.

I look into his eyes with a sudden, strange emotion, a need to speak. But my throat is raw, my tongue a swollen wad in my dry mouth.

No time for talk. We've got to get you out of here.

I cling to him like a baby as he pulls me to my feet and half-walks, half-drags me across the floor. If my legs are carrying me, they're doing it on their own. I can't feel them, have no sensation of movement except for the relative motion of the things around me.

134

A door looms, closer, slowly swings open, and we pass through into a corridor. Hammie's face seems to float out ahead of me, then suddenly hover at the tip of my nose, then float out again as we progress.

Through a half-open door I see the Dominos, slouched around a card table littered with reefers and gin bottles. Somehow, they don't see us as we make our laborious way down the impossibly long hallway.

We come to another door, and I see Inez Ravenswood recumbent on a chaise longue. Her shoes are off, and Geiger is there on his knees, painting her toenails. He blows delicately on them, then turns one monocled eye toward the door, seemingly looking right at me.

I panic, try to throw off Hammie's arms and make a run for it, but he holds me easily, puts a finger over my lips.

Shh. It's okay. They don't see you.

We make it out the back way. It's dark, and for a moment I'm upside down and the stars are below me, but then I realize it's the city lights, spread out like a shimmering blanket. I have my first coherent thought in days: *We must be in the hills.* I see a sign: Mulholland Drive.

Hammie keeps up an encouraging patter as we make our way around the side of the house to a high hedge. Behind it is the Packard, waiting at a lamppost like an old friend.

Look—I brought your car!

He opens the driver's side door, shoves me in and climbs in behind me, taking the wheel.

I'll drive. Here, you might need this.

He pushes the button on the steering column, and the little door under the dash swings out. But instead of a pistol fixed inside, there's a whiskey bottle.

Go ahead. Take it.

I take it, but I don't open it, just hold it against my belly. He kicks the engine to life and the tires spit gravel.

We careen down Mulholland, leaning into the Packard with every curve. Hammie seems to be watching me more than the road, but I'm too grateful for freedom to worry. I uncork the bottle and take a long, deep pull. The whiskey warms my throat, promises that all will soon be well. I think I can talk now, but I keep quiet, clutching the bottle, concentrating on the warmth that's spreading through me. I take another pull.

Hammie smiles his approval. *Save some for me.*

I hand him the bottle. He takes a pull, and I hear the Packard's tires squeal in protest. With every passing moment I feel clearer, more aware, but there's still a thick film between me and the world.

You don't look so good.

I find my voice: *That's funny. You're the prettiest thing I've ever seen.*

He laughs, hands back the bottle. The road seems to swoon away from us, the Packard rocking easily as it floats above the city.

Hammie eyes me pleasantly, as if at some great joke he wants to share.

Drugs. Water treatments. Isolation. Bright lights. No lights. Kicks and coddles. Now he's your pal, now he's the Devil...

I hear his words, but they make no sense to me.

Geiger works you over good, huh?

I'll say.

But he's nothing compared to the dames!

I lift the bottle in agreement. He takes it, drinks, passes it back.

A fleeting thought passes, that one of us should be watching the road. Hammie's eyes stay fixed on me, his face contorted into a death's-head grin.

The ringer...

How's that?

Hammie twitches the gold-banded ring finger of his left hand, clicking it against the top of the steering wheel.

The ring on your finger. The ring in your nose. The kiss like a ringer in a not-so-friendly poker game. The wringer they put you through...

Yeah, sure.

My own mother. He shakes his head at a long, bad memory. *She ran out on me when I was a kid. How about yours?*

Always traveling.

A-broad, huh?

136

We laugh hilariously, but the raucous sound in my ears suddenly turns me serious.

My father was a gardener. A good, honest man.

My father...

Hammie spits.

Of all the bitches in my life, my father turned out to be the biggest bitch of all.

The tires shriek. The Packard, no longer floating, swerves madly.

Take it easy!

There's no taking it easy, Buddy. Not on this road.

The car speeds faster. Hammie's hands tense on the wheel as he struggles to keep control.

Every twist is a twist of the knife. Every turn a turn of the screw.

I brace myself against the dashboard with my hands, letting the whiskey bottle drop. I hear it rolling between my feet, gurgling out its last swallows.

Slow down.

We're going all the way, pal. To the end of the line.

Slow down, I tell you!

The death's head grins wickedly, wrenching the wheel into another curve.

Worried about your cargo?

His words are strange, but there's something familiar in his tone, something I can't place.

What are you talking about?

What you've got in the trunk. Out of sight, out of mind, huh?

You're out of your head.

No more than you, pal. I've had my eye on you.

And then it clicks.

You're the voice on the phone!

That's right. Your shadow. Your constant companion. You see, we're twins, you and me.

I stare at him. The plastered-down hair, the penciled-in mustache, the dime store glasses—he's a cartoon. He mugs at me as if to emphasize how different we are.

Twins, I tell you. Two honest men—drowning in a world of deceit. Awash in lies. Swamped in corruption...

His good humor bleeds off, his manner agitated. The Packard, simpatico, bounces violently beneath us.

And the betrayal! In the eyes, in the lips, in the heart. And in the blood, pal, don't forget the blood!

I want to scream. What is he saying?

But the worst—the worst betrayal of all—

I try to shout. No! I don't want to hear it! Watch the road— watch the road! But the words won't come. I can only brace myself against the inevitable.

The mind! The betrayal of the mind!

I grab the wheel. The Packard careens madly, its tires barely clinging to the road. Hammie stamps the brakes, but we seem only to fly faster. He shouts in panic.

The brakes! Someone's cut the lines!

I yank on the hand brake but get no response.

The hand brake's out!

Hammie looks at me wildly, the wheel spinning in his hands.

Somebody wants me dead, York! Bad enough to kill both of us. Ask yourself—who profits? Who profits if we're dead?

If I know the answer, there's no time to speak it. The Packard leaves the road, floating for real now. A long, lazy arc, down, down into a void, not of blackness, but of sudden, blinding light.

-20-

I woke in a start, springing up, only to be knocked back again by a spike through my head. Weirdly colored blotches appeared before my eyes, and for a moment, the pain was chased away by a cloud of moths buzzing in my skull. Nausea welled up in me, but I was able to suppress it by squeezing my eyes shut and counting my breaths. When the feeling subsided, I opened my eyes to see a vague whiteness all around me. It was as if I was in a cocoon, or maybe just wrapped in a linen sheet, but when I pushed my hand against the whiteness, there was nothing there.

Slowly, things began to come into focus: an overhead light fixture, a vase full of flowers, a window. Two dark shapes hovered before the open sash, blocking the light. I tried to ease myself up, wincing at a knife of pain in my ribs. The shapes seemed to stir.

A familiar voice said, "Hey, look who's awake."

"Told ya. Like a rubber ball, this guy, always bounces back."

Guild and Lestrade. They floated toward me, coming in and out of focus. I tried to make some quip about the hospital being hard up for candy stripers, but it wouldn't come together.

"Hey, he's trying to talk."

They leaned over me, their looks all sympathetic interest.

"How ya feelin', sport?"

My answer came out dry and raspy. "Like I got tossed off a cliff in a washing machine."

Lestrade handed me a paper cup. In the staleness of my mouth the water had a foreign taste, but I gulped it down.

"Thanks."

"Doc says you got three cracked ribs and a fractured skull," Guild reported. "You been out a couple days, but you'll be all right."

Lestrade said, "I told the Doc it was lucky you landed on your head instead of your ass."

One chuckle and one cracked rib added up to a shiv-like pain.

"That's funny," I groaned. "How's the other guy?"

Guild frowned. "That's not so funny. He's dead."

The wind left me in a long, wheezing breath. I tried to think back, to pull something out of the haze. I remembered something about a hand brake.

"It was the brakes," I said. "Somebody tampered with the brakes."

Guild and Lestrade passed a dubious look.

"What?" I asked.

"You sure it wasn't all that booze?" Guild said.

"You were swimming in it."

"But I wasn't driving. Ravenswood was."

Another look.

"I don't think so," Guild said. "You were the one behind the wheel."

Images came back to me. The house on Mulholland. Geiger and his henchmen.

"Sure, I remember. Claude Geiger was holding me at a place on Mulholland, trying to get some information out of me. Ravenswood broke me out. I could barely walk. If he wasn't behind the wheel when you found us, he must have been thrown from the crash."

And another look.

"Come on, what gives? What are you two playing at?"

"What are *you* playing at, York?"

"I tell you, Ravenswood was driving!"

"He couldn't have been driving," Guild said. "We found his body stuffed in the trunk, some kind of fancy knife stuck through his heart."

The room seemed to spin around me. I heard myself shouting that Guild was a liar, felt myself fighting against the two cops as I struggled to get out of the bed. Then something wide and flat and hard came up and smacked me in the face, and for a few minutes the whole world was shoes, first four black ones shuffling about in a panic, then two white ones with low heels and a hushed, scolding voice that chased the black shoes away. Then sleep.

-21-

When I woke again the white sheet that enfolded me had turned to gray. No panic this time, no jumping up, just a slow, familiar return to consciousness. No mysteries in the blurs and shadows, just the simple gray-black of nighttime. But I heard something. Someone moving in the room.

My eye followed a shaft of yellow light that poured in from the half-open door. A woman bent over a metal cabinet. Hellen Vergos. She was holding a bottle of liquid, inspecting it under the light. She put it aside and picked up another bottle, checked the label, shook out three pills into her hand. Pinching one between thumb and forefinger, she held it up, peering closely at it.

"Hellen?"

Starting, she shunted the pills aside and turned on me a facile smile.

"You're awake!"

She bounced over to the bed and hugged me around the shoulders. It hurt.

"Easy, easy."

She eased. "I'm sorry. I'm just so glad to see you open your eyes."

She pecked me lightly on the forehead.

"Is that okay?"

"That's fine."

She sprinkled several more kisses over my face, then sat on the side of the bed, beaming at me.

After about a minute of that I said, "Maybe I should sell tickets."

She flushed, but kept the smile. "I'm just so happy to see you."

"I don't know why. Looks to me like I've fouled things up pretty good."

"Don't say that."

"I'm sorry about Hammie."

Her face clouded. Her fingers found a loose thread on the border of my blanket.

"It wasn't your fault."

"The cops seem to think it was."

"I know it wasn't."

I looked at her, but her eyes wouldn't meet mine.

"And what is that exactly? That you know."

That facile smile again. I'd never noticed it before.

"I know *you*." She placed her hand over my heart. Selling it. But I wasn't buying.

"Don't be so sure."

The hand retreated. "I knew Hammie, then. It was as if...How shall I say it? He was never happy in this world."

"You talk like it was suicide."

She turned away, her voice distant.

"Yes. Suicide. A long and painful dissolution."

"That got cut short by a very expensive knife."

She spun on me like I'd slapped her.

"Don't make a joke of it!"

"Who's joking? Somebody murders the love of your life—your brother, your boyfriend, whatever—and you're talking like he did it himself."

"You didn't know him. Hammie was self-destructive."

"Maybe. But somebody thought he was too slow about it."

She searched my face. "You don't think *I* had anything to do with it."

"No, just like I don't think you had anything to do with all those cute little drawings I keep finding."

"What drawings? What are you talking about?"

"The little ink doodles. The pig on the spit. The man in the spider web. I found a hundred of 'em in your apartment."

"In my apartment? You mean you—"

"That's right. It's called breaking and entering. One of my specialty services. No charge."

"How dare you!"

"Save it. What'd you think you were gonna do, gaslight me?"

"I don't know what you mean."

"You've seen the movie. Little tricks to get me talking to myself. Mysterious phone calls, anonymous threats, strange drawings."

"Those were Hammie's drawings. He was always doodling."

"Right, so I suppose he's the one who slipped one in my pocket, just after I happened to leave your place. Just like he stabbed himself in the back. Just like he killed Dahlia."

She tried to pull away from me, but I grabbed her by the wrist.

"You're talking crazy."

"Yeah, that's what I thought about Dahlia, last time I spoke to her. But I got to thinking, and her crazy talk started making sense."

"You're hurting my arm."

"Let it hurt. She said something about the Courthouse. Something I might find there that was a dime a dozen, but one was worth a million bucks."

"Dahlia was a drug addict. Why would you put stock in anything she said?"

"At first, I thought she was talking about the deed to Guy Pollone's place. But so what if Ravenswood owned it? What would that prove?"

"She was talking about the photographs, obviously."

"No, not the photos, and not that phony ram's horn. A birth certificate. Your birth certificate, Angel. With Col. Ravenswood listed as the father."

I'd struck a chord now, but she played it cool.

"I don't know what you're talking about."

"You thought Pollone had it, so you tipped Geiger off about the rendezvous on Mulholland. He'd get the photos and the hundred grand, and you'd get the certificate. A good deal all around. But something went wrong. Maybe Pollone tried to pull a fast one. Maybe he didn't realize what he had. That's why, when you heard Pollone was dead and the birth certificate didn't show, you hotfooted it over to his place. We almost bumped into each other, remember?"

"I don't remember any such thing!"

"Oh, but you'll remember that you didn't find it. Pollone didn't have it, after all. Probably he never even knew about it. So that left Dahlia."

She shook her head as if to blot it out, but I was on a roll.

"It was worth a million bucks to her, but so much more to you, Angel. So you killed her for it."

"That's a lie! She died of a drug overdose."

"Yeah. A specialty of yours, isn't it?"

She tried to break free, but I held her fast.

"What were you doing with those pills?"

"What pills?"

I pointed at the cabinet. "Those pills! Just now, when I woke up. What were you doing with them?"

"Nothing, I—"

"Better yet—what were you *going* to do with them?"

"I didn't—"

"I saw you. I saw you pour those pills into your hand."

She glanced at the door.

"Yell, and I'll break your arm."

Her voice became hushed. "You don't understand. I was checking them. Checking to make sure they matched the bottle."

She leaned close, conspiratorial. "You can't trust anyone."

"Yeah, that's what Hammie said."

"He was right. Even I let him down."

The schoolgirl act again, all sincerity and remorse. I resisted the urge to smack her across the chops. "Yeah. Something else Hammie said. Somebody wanted him dead."

"Nobody wanted Hammie dead. Not even Inez."

"No, not Inez. Two dead, rich husbands in one week might even raise the suspicions of the lugs at L.A.P.D."

She said very evenly, "Let go of me."

"'Who profits,' he said. 'Who profits if I'm dead?'"

"Stop it!"

"Who wanted more than anybody to keep Hammie out of Inez's clutches? Whose plans to marry rich went down in flames when it turned out she was a blood relation? Huh? But whose plans rose up again like a phoenix on the back of that birth certificate? Who wanted that piece of paper so bad she'd kill her own mother to get it?"

She collapsed on the bed, sobbing. I looked at her, feeling nothing.

"The sometime sister..."

Suddenly, she was all fury, flailing at me with everything she had.

"Lies! Lies!"

I fought her off, slapped her once good across the cheek. She grabbed for the phone, but I wrestled her for it.

"I know too much!" I hissed. "You want me dead, too!"

"No! You don't know what you're saying!"

There were voices murmuring down the corridor. She tried to scream, but my hand was across her mouth. I felt the phone's receiver hit me a glancing blow across the temple. I twisted it away from her, the cord becoming tangled around my hands. Tangled around her neck.

"It ends here!" I shouted. "It ends right here!"

She tried to scream again, but I had her by the neck. Knifes of pain cut through my ribs, but I gritted my teeth and clamped my hands tight. I squeezed until she couldn't scream, and I squeezed and squeezed until she became very still.

The voices in the corridor came louder, footsteps approaching fast.

My hands released her, rising up before my eyes, two red claws framing her still, ashen face.

"Hellen!"

And then they were on me.

-22-

The rest is a haze, but several points are clear enough. I was arrested, jailed, arraigned. The charge was murder. The plea— irrelevant. I'd killed. And I was going to pay for it.

Everyone said I was guilty. The prosecutor. The press. The crowds of people outside the courthouse. Just getting to the courthouse was like facing a firing squad, with the people shouting for my head and the flashbulbs going off like gunshots. The close quiet of my jail cell became my only comfort, and I longed to be locked away behind those sheltering walls and forgotten.

The court proceedings were confused, impenetrable, like a foreign movie somebody forgot to dub. There was a prosecuting attorney, a judge, a jury. There must have been counsel for the defense, but I don't remember him, nor anyone who spoke in my favor. The endless accusations and unanswerable questions overwhelmed my exhausted brain. The mute, owlish stares of the jury unnerved me.

The prosecutor summed up, pointing his finger at me like God's own judgment. Guilty! he said. And the jury echoed him, like a Greek chorus: Guilty! The judge, sitting so high above me I had to crane my neck to look up at him, pronounced the sentence: Death by electrocution. And may God have mercy on your soul. He brought his gavel down heavily, as if to smite me on the spot.

So I was guilty of murder. That much I understood. But who had I murdered? Was it Hammie, found in the trunk of my car with the horn-hilted dagger in his heart? His murder could only have happened after the crash, and I had no memory of it. Was it Hellen? I told myself no a thousand times. I couldn't have done that, not to her. But the dream of every kiss we shared was blotted out by the image of my hands around her throat. Maybe it was Col. Ravenswood, killed by the same knife as Hammie, the knife I thought I had put in a locker out of anyone's reach, even mine. Or maybe it was Dahlia. I'd been seen where the body was found. What did the D.A. care if I was guilty, as long as he could get a conviction?

Somehow, the jigsaw pieces have all come together, but the image I'm supposed to see has come up blank. I have committed a crime. I understand that. I accept the verdict. I even accept the sentence. But I should know who I am accused of killing. Somewhere, somehow, in the papers, in the courtroom, the victim's name must have rated a mention. Someone must have told me. Why can't I remember?

Something's wrong. Something's rotten here. Something's out of joint....

So now I wait, strapped to the chair in death's own sitting room, staring up at the clock's ghostly image, watching my appointment with the reaper tick, tick, tick closer—wanting, now that it's too late, to speak, to plead my case—not for innocence, but for a grain of understanding—trying to scream, chafing at the straps and manacles that bind me, struggling vainly to control my failing bowels.

Tick, tick, tick...

They throw the switch.

And then...

-23-

My mind is a white hot point at the center of an alien carcass that burns, jerks, goes rigid, its movements both painful and strangely far away. A billion sizzling wires penetrate every nerve ending, but it's only the sensation of an instant. A flash of exquisite completion, in which knife and wound and pain and scream are all one. But only a flash. Then nothing.

But not nothing. The physical world remains, but the thread of direct sensation is severed. The electric current coursing through my body is a vague memory. The ability to move these wan appendages a long-forgotten skill. I am still, silent, not seeing, hearing, or feeling, but aware, somehow, of everything around me. I seem to see without seeing the great moon of a clock, its glass cracked, its hands frozen at thirteen minutes to twelve. A room, all white tile and stainless steel. In one corner an ugly console of dials and switches. Two men in smocks, leaning over a table. And on the table another man. Dark, disheveled hair. Sunken eyes. Dressed in a hospital gown, his body strapped to the table. A large, rubber plug stuffed in his mouth. Something like oversized earmuffs attached to his temples.

Suddenly, a high-pitched beeping. I hear it without hearing, my ears dead but my sense of hearing somehow unnaturally keen. One of the men, dark-skinned, wearing corrective glasses with one lens blacked out, leans over the patient.

His heart's going into arrhythmia, Doctor!

The doctor's bullet-shaped head snaps up.

What? Impossible!

The machine wails.

He's flat-lining!

There's panic in the assistant's voice. The doctor pushes him aside, checks the machine, his eyes starting, the round dome of his brow knit in fury.

Get the Blue Team in here!

The assistant touches a button on the intercom.

Code Blue! Code Blue!

And I see beyond this room, to another. A square, windowless room with a sink and small refrigerator, where two black men in hospital scrubs sit at a card table, sipping coffee, playing a lazy game of dominos. An alarm sounds, and the excited voice comes over the intercom. The men bolt from their chairs, grabbing a mobile cart and racing down the corridor.

I see them all in the white tile room, working fast, holding a breathing apparatus over the patient's face, ripping open his gown to expose his chest, charging the defibrillator. They all look strangely familiar. But it is the man on the table, the patient, that I am interested in. I know him, and yet I do not know him. The face is waxy, the chin a stubbled blue. No mustache. No glasses. No hat. The hair neither slicked down nor even carelessly combed, but uneven, sticking out at all angles as if it had been attacked by a drunken barber. No gleam in the dead eyes. No cynical twitch of the pale lips. I stare at him, if staring, without eyes to see, is the word.

Is that me?

-24-

Two tabby kittens and a pink ball of yarn are tacked on the wall of a small, bare room. Twenty-eight little boxes are marked with black X's. The day is Friday. The month is November. The year is an improbably high, nonsensical number. Next to the calendar is a stainless steel mirror, screwed directly into the medicinal green wall. Below the mirror is an enamel wash basin with soap, toothbrush, and toothpaste. A damp washcloth is draped over the faucet to dry. Across from the basin is a small dressing cabinet, large enough to hold no more than a three-day change of clothes. Next to that is an iron bunk, its coarse blanket pulled over a mattress just two fingers thick. A naked bulb, caged like a blind, bald parrot, hangs from the ceiling, burning dimly and emitting a faint, plaintive buzz.

The room, in a word, is bleak, the view from its one barred window even bleaker: a brick wall, sooty red in color, thirty feet high, capped by a gray slate roof. Above the gray, a patch of blue sky offers the only hint of any world beyond. But that little patch of blue is all the mind needs. That world beyond, despite the high walls that block it out, exists. It's real, populous, and bustling. And the mind can ride that little patch of blue right over those walls, taking it wherever it wants to go.

Beyond those walls (miles away? years away?) there's the Ravenswood estate. The ivy-bearded parapets brood down on a lawn grown shaggy and leaf-strewn from neglect. A lone gardener clips disconsolately at an endless hedge. He pauses to watch the chauffeur bring the limousine up from the garage.

Inside the mansion is a room, also bleak, but in a very different way, with a carved four-poster bed and a clutter of books and movie paraphernalia. The heavy curtains are drawn back, the windows open, air and sunshine pouring in where they have not been known for years.

Two women in maid's uniforms, one standing on a stepladder, are stripping the walls bare of their solid plastering of movie posters: *The Big Sleep, The Glass Key, Murder My Sweet, The Blue Dahlia, The Maltese Falcon, The Thin Man.* One of the women hums a breezy tune. Both work carelessly, unmindful of how the aging paper rips in their hands.

The door swings open. And there's Hellen. Her neck is corseted in a rigid brace, giving her a birdlike erectness.

"What are you doing? Those belong to Mr. Ravenswood!"

The maid on the stepladder answers in a self-satisfied Cockney lilt.

"Missus Ravenswood said pull 'em down and burn 'em. The young master's comin' home and she don't want his head filled with no more nonsense."

To emphasize the point, she passes a nod at the other maid, who mirrors the gesture in approval.

Fuming, Hellen spins on her heel and stamps down the hallway. With a toss of her head, the maid on the ladder rips the middle out of *In a Lonely Place.*

Hellen tramps through the underpopulated halls, turning stiffly at every doorway, but the woman she is looking for has already left.

The long, black limousine glides easily through the winding hills of Brentwood. There, in the back seat, is Inez. Her alabaster face is impassive behind a sheer, black veil, her eyes even, focused on some distant object only she can see. One black-gloved hand lifts the veil as the other brings a perfumed cigarette up to her blood-red lips.

The limousine comes to a narrow drive and turns. The sign at the gate reads, "Angel of Mercy Sanitarium."

Within the dour walls of the sanitarium is a large, utilitarian space with bars over the windows, chipped tables, and worn sofas and chairs. People in bathrobes and house shoes shuffle about, sit, stand, some silent, some talking, either to themselves or others. There is music and games, lending a party-like air to the place, but

152

without the collective sense of a truly festive occasion, as if each attendee had been invited separately, each for his or her own secret, sad celebration.

There's Mr. Guild and Mr. Lestrade, playing a spirited game of checkers. Mr. Guild makes the pieces jump on the board as he haphazardly kings several men. Mr. Lestrade notes every move in a pad, using a strange matrix of jottings that make sense only to him. Mr. Fergus wanders about in aimless circles, muttering fearfully, a dinner tray clutched to his chest as if he is holding onto his very life. Mr. Pollone, catatonic, eyes blank and unblinking, stands propped in one corner like an umbrella. Over the nattering of a college football game on the radio a piano jangles tunelessly, the neat-looking man who sits at the keys playing to an imaginary crowd. A woman, her big, almond-shaped eyes staring and haunted, stands next to the piano, her hands clasped fretfully before her, her voice quavering to the tune of "No Regrets."

> *Left my home,*
> *My sunny clime,*
> *Spent my money,*
> *Every dime...*

And there, sitting on a sway-backed sofa, his cotton, hospital-issue pajamas wrapped in a two-hundred-dollar, monogrammed, silk dressing gown, his eyes fixed on the singer as if she and he are somewhere far, far away, is Hamlet Huffington Ravenswood III. That's me. Or some version of me. Some remembered self that I don't quite recognize. They call him Ham.

Mr. Fergus jostles him/Ham/me as he makes his endless circuit around the rec room, but Ham scarcely notices. His attention is fully on the woman called Dahlia, his eyes fixed on her as if she were the most glamorous woman he had ever seen, his ears attuned as if her song were the raptures of heaven itself. In one hand he clutches a pen. In his lap is a pad of paper, the top leaf adorned with a half-finished sketch of the singer as she might appear in the idyll of her dreams.

Sitting next to Ham, listening respectfully to Dahlia but taking no real interest as she frets at the fingers of her white gloves, is the nice lady who comes to visit him every week. He pretends not to know her just because he knows it hurts her. Hurting her makes him feel mean, which only makes him pretend all the harder that she isn't there. He can't understand why she always brings the gardener with her, or why the gardener always brings him flowers.

No regrets...no regrets!

When Dahlia finishes her song, the lady and her gardener applaud politely and she attempts to make small talk.

"That was very nice," she says to Ham, then nodding at the gardener.

"Very nice," the gardener says.

"Billie Holiday used to sing that song. Do you—do you remember when we would play her records?"

Ham frowns, darkening a line in his sketch with a ballpoint pen. The gardener clears his throat.

"Do you like the flowers we brought you?" she asks. "They're from our nursery. Lilies." She says the word with emphasis. "Do you know the name—Lily?"

Ham looks at the flowers disinterestedly, then, just as disinterestedly, at the lady. Slowly, almost imperceptibly, he shakes his head, his eyes looking past her at some distant, indefinable point.

A white glove goes to her mouth. The gardener puts his hands on her shoulders. The music begins again and an attendant gives a nod.

The gardener says something in the lady's ear. She nods in understanding and rises.

"We'll see you again next week," she says. "You be good. Take your medicine."

She seems to want to say something else, but she doesn't. Ham wouldn't respond anyway. She goes, and only after Ham is sure she won't look back does he turn to watch her retreat. His eyes narrow with disapproval at the familiar way the gardener pats the lady's shoulder with a consoling hand.

Something about that hand on that shoulder isn't right. Just like there is something about the lilies that isn't right. It's not that the flowers are ugly, it's just that...they should be something else. He plucks one and carries it over to Dahlia. She takes it, uncertainly at first, but then, with a slowly blooming smile, places it in her hair

The piano player, annoyed by this interruption, hits a jarring note, signaling Ham to sit back down. Ham sits, letting his mind idle as he waits for the piano player's fingers to wander back to their crooked tune.

Outside, just visible through the barred windows, Ham sees the black limousine pull up in the drive and disgorge the lithe figure of Inez Ravenswood. She ignores the people out on the lawn, although several call to her as if they know her. As she climbs the steps to the entrance she is met by the older couple, who are just on their way out. Their conversation is out of Ham's earshot, garbled anyway under the jangling of the out-of-tune piano, but it goes something like this:

"Well, well," Inez says. "If it isn't the Bailey-Ravenswood-Tanakas."

Although she stands several steps below the couple, she seems to look down on them, giving them a disdainful once-over. "And in your Sunday-go-to-meeting clothes. The tomato business must be good these days."

The gardener touches the lady's elbow. "Don't speak to her."

As if heeding his words but compelled to ignore them, she squares her shoulders and replies stiffly to Inez, "The produce business is very good, thank you." Then: "I see your profession still thrives."

Inez smiles as if at an insincere compliment.

"Ha. And how is the patient? Still pretending not to know you?"

The lady steps toward Inez, but her companion gently places himself between the two women. She looks at Inez with a hatred that Inez seems to relish.

"We'll see if the judge thinks he's pretending."

As the two women stare, each as if waiting for the other to crack, the gardener says something to his companion in Japanese. She says something back. They laugh, and as they brush past Inez, the haughty, amused look she so scrupulously cultivates withers from her face. Inez's eyes narrow as if taking aim on their retreating backs.

"A word to the wise, Lily," she says suddenly. Struck by the sound of her name on those lips, the older woman stops and turns to hear her. "H.H. always had a way of getting judges to think the way he wanted them to think. And so do I."

Inez whirls without sparing a second to take stock of any reply or reaction. She mounts the steps with uncharacteristic haste and pushes her way through the high wooden doors of the entrance. Once inside, she stops and lets the doors swing shut behind her. The cigarette in her hand goes reflexively to her lips and she sucks at it as if she means to inhale it flame and all.

"There's no smoking in the reception area, ma'am," a mop-wielding custodian informs her.

Haughty composure returns to her face. With a loud snort, she expels the nicotine through her nose, drops the cigarette on the still-wet floor, and extinguishes it with her toe. The custodian opens his mouth to protest, but Inez's frigid, insincere smile freezes the complaint in his throat.

After checking in at the desk, Inez is directed down the hallway to the rec room. She gazes down the brightly lit, sterilized corridor as if the voices that echo through it were uttering insult, and with a long gust of breath, she starts walking. Her heels resound on the polished floors, clacking like jackboots. She is dressed all in black, save for the shock of a red, silk scarf that cascades from her neck like the mark of a black widow. A pin, shaped in the abbreviated spiral of a hunting horn, glitters over her breast.

She is met at the door of the rec room by an attendant whose one visible eye droops lazily through its corrective lens. He listens closely over the din of the various activities as she speaks a word to him, then leads her to the sofa where Ham sits, listening raptly as Dahlia's song comes creaking to an end.

156

After waiting out Ham's enthusiastic applause, the attendant says, "Mr. Ravenswood, your mo—I mean, your *wife*—is here to see you."

Inez dismisses the attendant with a cold look, but when he turns to go, she stops him. She sweeps up the pot of flowers at Ham's elbow and thrusts them into the attendant's gut. He almost drops them, the dirt spilling onto his hospital whites. Anger narrows his one, visible eye, but he says nothing and goes.

"Hello Ham."

But Ham doesn't answer. With an awkward flourish of discordant notes, the piano player takes up the tune again and Dahlia sings. The song is rendered sad and hopeless in Dahlia's thin voice, and Ham grits his teeth, determined to control his emotions in front of Inez.

Inez doesn't see this, only that she is ignored. She takes the pad from Ham's unresisting hands, glances back and forth between the drawing and Dahlia. "Who's that supposed to be?"

She doesn't seem to expect an answer, and she doesn't get one. Her eye turns to the sofa, the empty space beside Ham, and she looks at it as she might at murky waters. She drops the pad onto the sofa, as if to test it. The pad neither sinks out of sight nor is devoured by vermin. She sits.

"Well, this is certainly dreary enough. For what you're paying for this place you could have a suite at the Roosevelt."

Ham pays her no mind, but her presence has electrified the atmosphere of the room. Mr. Fergus's aimless circuits have become tight circles, his eyes continuingly cutting in Inez's direction. The checker game between Mr. Guild and Mr. Lestrade becomes distracted and desultory. Even Mr. Pollone's unfocused gaze is now a fixed stare at the back of her neck. Inez, ever dismissive of the effects she creates, tugs at the fingers of her gloves, pausing when the piano hits a tinny note.

"Didn't they just play this song?"

Her gloves off, she stows them in her patent leather handbag. A silver cigarette case comes out.

"I don't suppose you'd get me an ashtray?"

Ham glances at her but doesn't move.

"I'll take that as a 'no.'"

She lights up.

For several minutes, Inez tries silence, chatter, the occasional probing question, but Ham does not respond to any of these tactics. When the piano player stumbles yet again through the familiar intro, Inez says, "Fourth time's the charm, I guess."

She sucks down another cigarette as Dahlia sings.

I took aim for the heart—
Always aim for the heart...

"Do you remember arguing about this song? You said 'aim for the heart' meant she trusted in love. I said it meant she shot the bastard."

No regrets...no regrets!

Agitated, Ham takes up the note pad, clicks the ball-point pen, adds some shading under one cheekbone.

"Still not talking, eh?" She stands, holds out a hand. "Come. Let's go see the Doctor."

Ham eyes her warily, but she holds her pose.

"You can bring your pad. Come. Come."

He looks at the hand, takes it in a childlike grip. For a moment, she seems warm, almost motherly. But as she leads him toward the door she pauses at the piano, as if in afterthought, and looks at Dahlia. Like a mouse closed up in a fist, Dahlia's song squeaks to silence. The piano player's fingers go still.

"And you really thought," Inez says to her, "that you had a hold on the old man."

That's all. Just those words, and she leads Ham away. He goes meekly but feels himself roiled with hate. Of all the reasons he has to despise her, it is this off-handed cruelty that he despises most.

-25-

Inez goes into the doctor's office first, leaving Ham sitting in the receiving area under the watchful eye of the secretary. The doctor's door is shut, the voices behind it muffled, but Ham can easily distinguish the speakers. Dr. Geiger does most of the talking, his jovial tone, like that of a popular lecturer, lilting high above Inez's bored, laconic sentences. Ham finds that if he listens closely enough, he can make out some of the words.

They're talking about me, or someone like me, or someone, at least, with a similar name. Surely, several different people, and yet supposedly all one. At least, that's what Dr. Geiger says. The diagnosis sounds impressive: Affective personality disorder with bipolar, manic-depressive tendencies and episodes of psychosis. But the story is simple enough. A difficult childhood, issues of abandonment, depression, retreat into fantasy. Anyone could understand it.

"You're not listening in, are you?" the secretary says in an accusing tone.

Ham shakes his head in a solemn no.

The secretary watches him a few minutes, clearly bored. There is nothing on her desk, seemingly nothing for her to do. She picks at a hangnail, opens a desk drawer and pretends not to be checking her lipstick in a mirror she has concealed there. She even takes a moment to admire the ruby-like nails of an immaculate pedicure that shows through her open-toed pumps. Throughout all of this, she keeps glancing at the clock, and Ham notices that it is almost twelve. Is it like that other clock, the one that keeps appearing to him, that never seems to reach midnight? But no, it's not midnight, it's broad daylight out. And the clock does move. Now twelve o'clock. Now after.

"You'll sit here quietly, won't you?" the secretary suddenly says.

Ham gives her a slow, sincere nod. It seems to satisfy her. She takes a brown paper bag out of her drawer, and with a last warning that Ham must sit quietly, she goes.

Immediately, Ham is at the Doctor's door. Peering through the keyhole, he can see and hear everything.

Inez sits in a Queen Anne chair before Dr. Geiger's carved mahogany desk, her legs crossed at the knees, one raised foot rhythmmically tapping the air. Geiger paces before her, passing back and forth through the brilliant light that pours in through the French doors that open out onto the sanitarium grounds. Geiger, in his accented English, talks animatedly, happily, as if pleased by his subject but even more pleased to have Inez as his captive audience.

"A truly, truly fascinating case."

Inez, as if to show that she finds it anything but fascinating, lights up another cigarette. Geiger scarcely notices, too caught up in his lecture.

"In the guise of this York, this gumshoe, young Hamlet—or 'Ham,' as you call him, 'Hammie' in his fantasies—became an investigator into the mystery of his own shattered life. What confused and overwhelmed his own delicate mind, the hard-boiled Ellis York was able to handle with aplomb. Or so he hoped."

Geiger chuckles, fiddles with his monocle as if lost in a moment's reverie. "Yes, so he hoped..."

If he's trying to garner a prompt from Inez, he doesn't get one. She responds only with a blue cloud from her perfumed cigarette.

"You see," he continues, "this York, unfortunately, is not much of a detective. For all his bluster, the two-fisted war hero still had the soul of the frail, 4-F washout who conjured him—blundering about town, getting drunk, picking fights with club bouncers and house servants. The more he investigated, it seems, the less he understood. You can imagine the responses he got, wandering from bar to bar with a photo of himself, asking everyone he met if they had seen him." Geiger shakes his head, looking both sad and amused. "And when he finally did 'crack the case,' as they

160

say...Well. Imagine sweet, innocent Hellen Vergos as a murderess..."

Geiger chuckles again, throwing a coy look at Inez as she flicks a stray scrap of tobacco from her finger. He clears his throat.

"Think of the state of mind of a sheltered young man, a man with deep issues of parental abandonment and betrayal, comfortable only within his own fantasies, who thinks he has won the love of the most beautiful woman in the world."

Geiger pauses ostentatiously, appraising Inez with an oily gaze. "Yes, the most beautiful woman."

"That's a vile phrase."

Geiger nods. "Perhaps you'd prefer to think of it as ironic."

From the angle of the keyhole, the side of Inez's face is just visible, but the smile is plain enough: coldly hostile but not deigning to engage, like a panther who observes a mouse crossing her path but isn't particularly hungry.

"Go on."

"By all means. As I was saying, our young man falls in love with this seemingly perfect creature. With this image of woman more vivid than anything he has seen or imagined, even in the movies, because she is real. His life is transformed. Where once all was bleakness, now there is hope, where once darkness, now light. His life becomes, for him, as perfect as the happy ending of a Hollywood musical. Even he can't quite believe it is real. And then, this new reality, this life-as-dream, is shattered. This most beautiful woman is stolen away by his own father. Bleakness again. A deep, deep depression, deeper even, than the depression he had felt when his mother abandoned him. You remember that, of course. She was driven away by her husband's incessant philandering."

"It rings a bell. Lounge singers, wasn't it?"

"Among others. To continue. Our young man has lost one love. Two, if you count his mother. But then, miraculously, he finds love again—true love, this time, love based not on fantasy or dependence but on friendship and mutual interest—love with a girl he has known since childhood. Again, like a Hollywood movie. You know. The ones where the hero fails to achieve happiness with the woman he believes he is in love with, only to find that true love has been under his nose all along."

"Yes. If she'd only ever thought of taking off those darned glasses before, they might have avoided the whole thing."

Geiger laughs. "Exactly. So now, this young man truly has found the woman of his dreams. But then, incredibly, like some perverse *deus ex machina* from a Greek play, his father steals her too, in a sense, with the revelation of his paternity. The woman our young man had come to think of as the love of his life is, in actuality, his own half-sister."

"How Oedipal."

"Textbook. He becomes consumed with violent fantasies and the desire for revenge. For his father, he imagines all sorts of extravagant deaths, even murder at his own hands. For his new mother figure he imagines—no, not rape—what shall I call it? Sexual dominion..."

Geiger drifts a moment, lost in scientific reverie, perhaps, as his eyes languish over Inez's form. She sniffs. Coming back to himself, he gives a dramatic frown.

"Ham's darkest wishes—for his father's death, for his stepmother's hand in marriage—precipitously come true. But the guilt is too much."

Geiger plants himself in front of Inez, leaning back against his desk, trying to draw her in with his own fascination.

"He snaps. What, to this point, has been a borderline personality, now succumbs to true psychosis. But a psychosis of his own unique character. A psychosis purely informed by movies."

"*The Wizard of Oz*, I suppose."

Geiger affects an exaggerated, close-lipped smile. "No. Murder mysteries. Detective stories. Don't you find that appropriate? So immersed is he in these movies, these *films noirs*, that he can only make sense of the outrageous occurrences in his life through the lens of Hollywood. In his fantasy, there were roles for each of us— he the hard-boiled detective, his deceased father the ambiguous bestower of the quest, I the criminal mastermind, you and Hellen the *femmes fatales*, even poor Dahlia, with her never-ending song, a tragic torch singer."

162

"Yes, I caught her act in the rec room. I saw Guy and Freddie, too. You know, it's too bad the old man is dead. Without his enemies and ex-lovers, what will you do for patients?"

"Enough with the jokes," Geiger says, his neck reddening above the collar. "I'm trying to explain something."

Inez blows a smoke ring that seems aimed to encircle Geiger's nose. He bats it away.

"Have you no scientific curiosity!"

Inez makes no response. The red of Geiger's neck has risen to his eyebrows, but he cools suddenly, affecting a patient smile. He nods at the pin that sparkles on her breast.

"Not even about the ram's horn?"

At the mention of the ram's horn, Ham presses himself more tightly against the keyhole, cups one ear with his hand. There is something about that. Something about a ram's horn that has been nagging at him, something that he must understand.

Inez says, "I'll bite. What is it?"

Geiger shrugs, in control again. "A prize. A weapon. A female adornment... Symbolically, the horn of a ram is both masculine and feminine, phallic yet curved, representing both the male's power and the female's...voluptuousness."

Another oily look. He seems to be trying to stare Inez down in some way, to establish some dominance over her. His eyes drift down her form, down her crossed leg, to her foot, where one shoe dangles carelessly from her toes, exposing the seductive curve of her instep.

Geiger swallows, his mouth gone dry. In the momentary silence, Inez doesn't deign to look at him. "And then," he continues, his voice straining for a casual note, "there is the myth of Aries. You may remember the story from your school days. The ram of the Zodiac. The Golden Fleece. Something about wicked Queen Ino and her two unfortunate step children...."

Inez flicks a stubby grub of ash onto Geiger's plush Persian carpet. For a moment, there is murder is in his eyes, but that gives way to a calculated expression of contempt.

"To think I once took you for a psychologist."

"Oh, I still am, Claude. I've just learned to make it pay."

The dangling shoe falls from Inez's foot. Geiger genuflects to retrieve it, taking a loving sniff of its interior before replacing it over her toes and heel. In the battle between them Inez revels in her superior position, but Geiger looks up at her in a way that reveals calculation rather than retreat.

"We'll soon see."

Out of patience now, Inez stands suddenly and stubs her cigarette out in the ashtray on Geiger's desk.

"Look, Claude, I'm here for one reason, and one reason only. All I want to know is whether we can pass Ham off as sane and competent. The hearing is Monday, and unless he and I can walk into that courtroom looking something like man and wife, Little Miss Sunshine and her lawyer will have the marriage annulled."

At the door, Ham fidgets with nervous excitement.

Geiger is standing now, facing Inez with a bland smile.

"I don't know why you're so jolly," Inez says. "If my gravy train derails, so does yours."

Geiger fans his hands up and down in a calming gesture. "My dear, I assure you, Hamlet is quite sane. My treatment has proven an unqualified success."

Inez snorts. "That's rich. Your 'treatment' almost killed him."

"Nevertheless." Geiger's eyes are narrowed, his jaw tensed. "It was unwise of you to file that lawsuit against me. We had a deal."

A moment passes in which the room seems to expand with pressure, then suddenly deflate. Inez eases up to Geiger's side, takes his arm. Her voice is all supplication.

"I know, it was foolish of me. When I heard Ham almost died, the thought of everything going to that, that half-caste, just made me—Well, what can I say? I panicked."

She gazes penitently up into Geiger's eyes, somehow making herself look small and vulnerable. Her foot finds its way out of her shoe again and massages Geiger's ankle.

"After all," she croons. "I did withdraw the lawsuit. Can't you forgive me?"

If her act is getting through to Geiger, he is able to cover. His voice is steady, in control. "Certainly, my dear. But now there is a new deal. As I said, Ham is sane, but he's far from well. He won't be going home."

Inez plants both feet firmly on the floor.

"What do you mean?"

"Young Ravenswood has proven himself very shrewd, in a way. He understands his need for care. But more importantly, he understands how to ensure that he gets it—without your interference."

"What are you talking about?"

"I'm talking about a lot of things. Security. Prestige. Prominence among one's peers. Even a personal sense of well-being. There are so many intangibles involved..."

"Stop this ridiculous cat-and-mouse!"

"My dear, there's no need to get emotional."

"Then talk straight."

"Of course. You're an objectivist. You like facts. Very well. Here are some facts. That fortune you crave, that house you live in, even that magnificent car you arrived in. The fact is that they all are assets of a new mental health foundation, with me at the helm and Ham, as you call him, as my number one patient."

Ham puzzles over these words. There is something familiar there. Something he should know about. Inez seems completely taken by surprise.

"You're joking. No court would approve that. It's unethical."

"Please. That word is an abomination on those pretty lips of yours. Besides, it is done. Already we have a charter, a distinguished board of trustees—including two judges, I might add—and, of course..."

Geiger takes a bow. "A Director of Clinical Research."

Inez is stunned. Still at the door, Ham smiles, sharing in the Doctor's triumph over her. She seems ready to collapse, and Geiger, like a boxer smelling blood, goes in for the knockout blow.

"Naturally, Col. Ravenswood's will shall be honored. As a nonprofit organization with the usual budgetary constraints, we may have to curtail your privileges somewhat, but I assure you that your allowance will remain untouched. Most of the house will be converted to office space and treatment rooms. The suite you presently occupy will better serve as my own quarters, I think, but I'll allow you a private room. Something similar to that of the patients, perhaps."

Inez sways on her feet, but Geiger steadies her, taking her in his arms.

"Never fear, my sweet. I'll take care of you. As my wife, if you like. Since your current marriage seems unlikely to last. If not, perhaps you'd like to return as my employee."

He leans in for a kiss, but she turns her face away, staring, wide-eyed. He ignores the rebuff, burying his face in the fragrant curve of her neck. She moves one hand mysteriously across her breast, up then down, and Geiger jerks away from her, rubbing the back of his hand.

"That was a childish trick!"

If Inez fears his anger she shows no sign of it. She stands her ground, her gaze haughty, penetrating.

"You wondered how I managed to dispose of the Colonel so neatly," she says. "Well. I picked up a few things from my years in medicine."

She coolly replaces the glittering pin above her breast. Geiger gapes at it, confused, then, as his knees begin to shake, with dawning understanding. He grips the desk for support.

"It works rather quickly, doesn't it?" Inez observes. "You'll feel lightheaded at first. Then a tingling in your fingers. Maybe a taste of metal in your mouth. Numbness. Shortness of breath. And then..."

She shrugs.

Geiger lurches to his knees, grips Inez by the wrist. She makes no attempt to pull away.

"I hate to lose, Claude. But if I must lose, I refuse to lose alone."

Gasping now for breath, Geiger grips her wrist tighter, attempts to pull himself to his feet. She smiles down at him, confidently at first, but he's not going fast enough. His grip is too firm, his eyes too intent. Inez tries to pull her wrist free, but he holds on. His foaming lips try to form words.

166

He can't get to his feet, but he manages to pull Inez downward, his face close to hers. His voice faltering, he rasps out his last words.

"No...not alone..."

There is a flash of metal. A retractable blade springs from Geiger's sleeve, and before Inez can react he plunges it into her, pinning her like a prize butterfly.

Inez emits a long, hollow gasp and sinks to the floor. Locked in their death embrace, their faces inches apart, they stare into each other's eyes as the life drains away.

-26-

The door clicks. Soft, hesitant footsteps.

Ham stands over them, looking into their dead eyes, watching the expanding pool of red that turns black in the carpet. He stares at them a long time. Then, as if remembering something long forgotten, he reaches into the pocket of his silk gown. He pulls out a crumpled fedora.

He looks at it a moment, as if wondering where it came from. There is a folded square of paper in the hatband. He unfolds it once, twice. A black ink sketch on white paper. A man in a fedora, like the one Ham has in his hand, stands with a smoking gun over two bodies, a man and a woman, little X's where their eyes should be. The picture makes Ham smile.

He places the fedora on the back of his crown, as if just to try it. Tugs it low over his eyes. He smiles again, gazing around him as if the whole world had gone black and white, like the pen-and-ink sketch in his hand. Cocking an ear, he listens to the silence in the room, hearkening to some unheard voice.

Sometimes gifts come in not-so-neat packages. And sometimes you can't solve a case with a magnifying glass and a deerstalker cap...

He looks again at the bodies.

What matters is the bad guys get theirs and the good guys come out on top.

He nods grimly, lets the sketch flutter to the floor between the bodies. A faint clamor draws his attention to the French doors. The green lawn is shrouded in gray, and a misting rain has sent everyone scurrying inside. He pushes the doors open and lets the damp air in, watching as the gray mist gathers around his feet. A trench coat on a rack near Geiger's desk catches his eye. He takes it down, finds the armholes, and lets the bulky garment settle around his shoulders. It feels good on him. Without a backward glance, he steps out into the rain. He hikes up the collar of the coat against the chill and walks across the lawn to the rain-slicked drive. His footsteps create a lonely echo on the cobblestones.

For the other guy's sins we always want justice. For our own transgressions—well, we'll settle for mercy...

In the swirling mists ahead, under a haloed streetlamp, a two-door coupe comes to a stop. An umbrella emerges, shielding a female figure. She comes toward him with small, quick steps.

Mercy. That's one commodity you can't make or buy or even steal. Sometimes you can only beg for it...

The woman stops. She lifts the umbrella's dripping brim to reveal a face framed in dark hair above a high, corseting collar. It's Hellen.

But sometimes...

Hi, Big Brother.

Her eyes take in the fedora, the ill-fitting coat, but her face is kind and forgiving. Like a sheepish boy, he pulls the hat from his head.

Hi, Sis.

She smiles, takes his arm, the umbrella falling to her side. They walk into the gathering night, shadows melting into the rain.

Sometimes you don't even have to ask...

THE END

About the Author

Michael Compton writes screenplays, novels, and short stories.
With his wife Sherry, he co-wrote and executive produced
the 2011 thriller *Carjacked*. He is currently collaborating on a
graphic novel, *Inferno-2033*.

Michael's scholarly work includes materials for the forthcoming
scholastic edition of J.D. Salinger's *Three Early Stories*,
published by the Devault-Graves Agency.

He teaches English and screenwriting at
The University of Memphis.

With the assistance of his dog Ike,
Michael blogs on movies and media at

www.ikeandmikeblog.com

Follow him on Twitter @ikeandmikeblog

~ ~ ~

A portion of all Michael & Sherry's earnings
goes to animal rescue and
spaying/neutering.